T A S H I N   R E Z A

Tashin Reza was born in a small village of North Dinajpur district of West Bengal. He is a peace loving and a self-dependent person. He values self-respect highly. He loves listening to music and reading novels. He is a good observer.

He has completed his post-graduation in pharmacy from a renowned college under Sikkim University. Presently, he is working as a drug safety associate in a US based company in Karnataka. He spends his leisure time in writing.

So far his work includes Love is a necessary evil and She lives in me.

'The volatile feeling' a novella is his third work in the literature world. You can get in touch with him in Facebook at www.facebook.com/tashin.reza, also you can email him at tashin786@gmail.com

THE VOLATILE FEELING

TASHIN REZA

ANJUMAN
PRAKASHAN

Published By

ANJUMAN PRAKASHAN

942, Mutthiganj, Prayagraj, 211003

Website - anjumanpublication.com

E-Mail - contact@anjumanpublication.com

First published by Anjuman Prakashan in 2019

Copyright © 2019 Anjuman Prakashan

Copyright Text © 2019 Jimil Patel

Typeset & Cover : Anjuman Prakashan, Prayagraj

ISBN : 978-93-88556-41-5

Dedicated to my friends

CONTENTS

ACKNOWLEDGEMENT

I would like to thank Sam Brian for his support and encouragement. I would like to thank all my friends for their valuable support in building this story. My especial gratitude goes to my college friends Pragati Maiti, Biswaraj Paul, Anirban Chakraborty, Soumen Nandi, Arijit Singha, Robin Roy, Subho Ghosh for their encouragement.

Lastly, I would like to extend my gratitude to everyone who either directly or indirectly has helped me to build this story.

CHAPTER ONE

The birds' morning chirping had stopped as the sun tried to push its rays through the thin layer of fog on the land of Meghalaya. The daily work of the people had begun. The paper-boy had delivered the newspapers to his assigned doors. On the cover of the paper that day was Sana, a girl from a small town of Meghalaya, who had been recognized for her outstanding results at her higher secondary school. Sana had scored the second highest mark in the entire state of Meghalaya, but she was still in bed when Piyali, a close friend of hers, went to her room with the paper in her hands. In the 90s, having your name appear in the daily was like getting a carrier in Bollywood.

"Get up!" Piyali ordered as she opened her window wide walking around the room. The morning sun rays brightened the room. Sana tried to open her eyes but her reaction to the light was too sensitive, so she kept her eyes closed. Piyali then pulled out the thin blanket she used to cover her body.

"What's wrong Piyali?" Sana asked in a dizzy voice, putting her face against her pillow. "Let me sleep!"

Sana was enjoying a sound slumber after getting her results the day before. She was happy and felt that her hard work had come to fruition. However, she did not yet know her name had appeared in the paper and Piyali wanted to surprise her with the news.

Piyali too had scored good marks, but she was not in the list of top three highest-achieving students.

"Look at it," Piyali said bringing the paper closer to her face, close enough to blur the focus point of her lens.

Sana snatched the newspaper and kept it aside. "You know I don't read newspapers."

Piyali wanted her to look at it.

"You should refer to a newspaper. Didn't our teacher used to tell us to read a newspaper?"

Every Indian student must have faced at least one suggestion from a teacher in their lifetime. *Read English newspaper.*

Sana forced her eyes wide open and looked for what Piyali had given her the paper for.

"Oh, what am I looking for?" She asked as she jumped out of her bed. "How… I mean, how can my name be here?"

The real warmth of seeing her name in the newspaper came later. The news skyrocketed the 5HT level of her brain and the pleasure she felt was visible on her face and through her excitement.

Sana and Piyali had been childhood friends. They had always shared their things freely with each other—a sign of pure friendship. Here, I chose the word "pure" to show their affection for one another. Whatever the extent of intimacy is between two girls, there will always be a phase when one becomes jealous of the other. This jealousy differs from individual to individual and is natural.

Sana took the paper and went to her mom. She stopped in the kitchen where her mom was busy preparing breakfast.

"Mom," she said, and moved closer. "Look, they have announced my name in the newspaper."

There was a bright smile on her mom's face. It thrilled her. She held Sana's arm and added, "I had already seen this in your hard work. I am so proud of you."

Sana remained silent; her heart beating fast with the excitement.

"Your dad will also be happy," her mom said as she stirred the milk on the gas oven "Keep the paper on the table. Let him come and get the surprise."

Sana left the newspaper on the table and went back to her room. Piyali was still sitting on her bed.

"So, what's the plan now?" Piyali asked. "We should enjoy this success."

"A movie or a late-night show," Sana said.

In those days, watching a movie in a cinema hall was like a great party in a pub. However, a late-night movie was more fascinating because their parents never allowed them to go to the cinema at night; however, Sana knew that they would not turn her request down this time. Sometimes, doing forbidden things gives more enjoyment.

In the evening, they got permission to go to the movie after telling their parents that they would be accompanied by many other friends.

They arrived at the cinema half an hour prior to the beginning of the movie and waited outside the hall. Looking around, they noticed that people had parked their bikes on one corner and there was a big queue in the line for men. Fortunately, the ladies' line was short and they were able to quickly buy their ticket. We have always given girls in India the privilege of space when a crowd is gathering.

"Look at him," Piyali said, pointing out the guy in blue jeans and a white shirt. "He's damn hot."

"Not as much as you think," Sana said. "Don't keep on looking at him. If he realizes, he may start following you."

"Don't worry. I'm not planning on talking to him," Piyali said. "I think it's time we enter the cinema hall."

"Wait just a few days more. You will meet many hot guys in college," Sana said as she walked towards the gate.

The phase after school and before joining college is so exciting for every individual.

"I am too excited about college," Piyali said. "Just like school days, I will not choose a guy based on how good he is in his studies."

"What parameter are you going to check then?" Sana asked, raising her eyebrow.

"The priority is that he should be tall. Second, he should not have any previous girlfriends," Piyali said.

"You mean you need a freshman," Sana said.

"Being fresh myself, why should I expect a used one?" Piyali said and laughed.

"Now stop your rubbish talks and let's get in," Sana said.

They went inside and sat down. A moment later, Piyali forgot the hot guy she was looking at as her full concentration penetrated into the story of the movie.

*****

"We cannot let you go that far for your studies," Piyali's mom told her when she asked about her admission to Meghalaya technical institute (MTI) - a college about eighty-five kilometers from her home.

Piyali hailed from an orthodox family, where rules and rituals were more important than anything in life. Many rules bound her. She never wanted to live life encapsulated with restrictions. Although it was a burden in her life, she had to obey her parents and she was restricted from eating non-veg foods. Every morning, she had to wake up early because her parents wanted her to, and the first activity she had to do was to pray in front of the temple, which was attached to her house. She was a firm believer of God, albeit not through prayers or visiting temples; she believed in God by doing good deeds. Every year, her parents made a trip to temples to a different corner of the country and they bound her to go with them.

"But I want to continue my studies, mom," she said in a sad tone.

"A hostel is not a good place for our family. So far, none of us have been in a hostel. You need to check out the colleges nearby," her mom said.

"I want to pursue a BSc and here none of the colleges offer a BSc degree," she said.

"I don't have an answer to your query. Ask your dad," she said and walked away.

Piyali remained seated. She did not know what she could do that get her parents to allow her to study away from home. She had discussed with Sana and both had planned to take admission in the same college to pursue their degree.

It was not only for the degree, but Piyali wanted freedom in her life, which she could only achieve if she studied away from her home. She called Sana to her home as she had decided to take the issue to her dad, and she knew Sana could support her in the best possible way.

Sana and Piyali sat on the sofa. Opposite to them sat Piyali's dad. Her father's look was furious. It seemed he has never smiled in his life. He was so busy with rules, ritual, religion, and gods that he had forgotten to enjoy life. For him, life meant prayers and sticking to the rules.

He was so strict that he barely interacted with his own daughter. It always scared Piyali to talk to him.

"I want to further my studies," Piyali said while pressing her left hand with her right in fear.

"I have talked with the MLA; he will get you admitted here to the government college," her dad said. "It is near and you can go from home."

"This college is college only for the sake of a name," Piyali said pressing her hand harder. "And they do not offer the course I want to take up."

"Your mother told me everything. You are not going away from home. That is my final saying," he said in a stern voice.

"Uncle we both want to go for MTI. Since childhood we have helped each other and so we prefer that college. Regarding admission, I have talked with one of my friend who will help us," Sana said.

Piyali's dad remained silent. There was no change in his facial expression and this was the reason Sana always denied meeting Piyali's father.

"Most of the students who have passed out from MTI are now somewhere in the different corner of the country, earning a good salary," Sana said.

"Look Sana, you can go ahead but please don't brainwash my daughter's mind," he said and went away. "Do not try to be more than a friend to Piyali."

It surprised Sana to listen to such words. She had always planned everything with Piyali. It was not her selfish wish to take Sana with her for the company but it was Piyali's desire.

Sana stood and walked out.

This hurt Piyali. It was an embarrassing situation for her. She had called her to support her and now it embarrassed Sana.

"Sana," Piyali called out. "I am sorry. Please wait."

Sana did not stop. She walked back to her home.

There was something that changed Piyali, gave her courage. She entered her room and cried. She had never expected that her dad would insult her friend to this extent. She felt low for the act of her father. This situation put her under depression and she gave up food. It was after three days when his father agreed to send her with Sana.

CHAPTER TWO

Sana and Piyali finally were in the hostel. They could successfully get admitted for Bsc in the college of their desire- MTI.

It had been tough for Sana to leave her home. She had always enjoyed the company of her parents. The excitement of the hostel was ruined with the depression on the day of leaving her house. She could see tears in her mom's eyes and it hurt her more.

Every parent loves their child unconditionally, but it is not the same for every individual. Unconditional love becomes a barrier while going away from home and there are hundreds of students who have failed to stay away from home only for this reason.

Unlike Sana, Piyali did not have a family attachment, so it was not a tough situation for her. Though she always wanted to be away from home while leaving the home for her new college she could feel the 'missing' growing in her. She had felt the pain before leaving. Value of the home is best understood by the people who pursue their education staying in a hostel.

"Are you ready?" Sana asked.

It was the first day of their college. They were still in their room. The college was at a distance of three kilometers but it provided them with a bus facility.

"Yeah, almost done," Piyali said standing with the mirror on her hand and looking if anything was needed more on her face.

"Enough Piyali, no one will propose you on the very first day," Sana said.

"I want none proposal on the first day," Piyali said smiling.

They left the room and walked to the spot where the bus would arrive. They had dressed in salwar and with light makeup. It had been so demanding for them to use makeup while going for their classes as their school forbade using makeup during class days.

Waiting for a while the bus arrived, and they got into it. There were many guys and girls. Few were talking something that was not audible. While they walked towards the back of the bus, guys starred at them. They knew it and Piyali kind of liked it.

"We will take this seat," Piyali said and sat. Sana moved to her and sat with her.

Everyone looked decent. Few people talked about introducing each other. It was their first-day college and every one of them was unknown to each other.

In fifteen minutes they reached the college. Slowly they walked to their allotted classroom. Every four or five people were introducing to each other. It was not the pre-made group. They grouped up according to the people they felt have a similarity in their thoughts and belief.

The class began with the entry of a young lecturer who seems to be more like a student. He started the class by introducing himself and then the introduction of all the candidates began.

"Look at the second last bench," Sana said. Sana had seen that guy long ago before the class and his looks and personality appeared to be likable by Piyali.

Piyali turned and took a quick look. "He is so cute," she said. I should talk to him after class.

"Never try to do it," Sana said. "If you talk first, they may miss judge you. When a guy approaches a girl, us calls it is like but the same thing when a girl does it leads to judging her character by the people around the guy."

"You think too much Sana," Piyali said. "Need to book before someone approaches. Guys are so stupid. They accept a proposal from any girl and I hate this habit."

Sana laughed silently putting her head on the desk to avoid getting sighted by the lecturer who was throwing knowledge and philosophy filled with do's and don'ts.

"Just stare, don't drag him to your bed in your thoughts," Sana said making a face.

"Shut up, you better find someone," Piyali said giggling.

"You see that guy sitting in the 2nd last desk," Sana said.

Piyali turned and look. She did not get why Sana called her to look at him. She thought Sana might be interested in him but Sana was a hard girl to get wavy by looks.

"Yeah," Piyali said. "What's special?"

"Group of girls was discussing him. Someone called him chocolate boy," Sana said.

"Chocolate," Piyali laughed keeping her hand on her mouth.

They did not know why he was given such a name. It was their first day, and they did not even bother to know.

***

The day ended. Sana and Piyali left the college and walked towards the gate. They were discussing the class and the upcoming subjects they had to study.

"Look to the right?" Piyali said seeing a girl surrounded with few boys. The appearance of the girl gave a look of the first-year student. It is quite easier to predict a person who comes to a new city by her appearance.

"What is happening?" Sana asked. She could see the guys were asking her something, and she was afraid. The guys laughed out loud. Sana and Piyali did not know what was happening.

"I think she is in trouble. Should we go?" Piyali said and stopped walking.

"We may be in trouble. Let's go back to the hostel. We know nothing about this college," Sana said and pulled Piyali to walk.

"Wait," Piyali said. She could see one boy getting closer to the girl. "This is not right."

Piyali left her hand and walked towards the girl. Sana followed her.

"Hi," Piyali said to the group.

Everyone's attention was now on Piyali and Sana.

"How can we help you madam?" two boys of the group proposed.

"We came to take her," Piyali said pointing the victim girl. She did not let her fear display on her face. She was confident. No one could look at her and say she was new to the college.

"Why? Are you her mom?" one boy asked giggling. "But I have never spent a night with you. Guys, did any of you make her mother?" Everyone laughed with this comment.

Sana could see the situation was worsening. She was afraid. She could not think the next step to get out of the issue.

"We want none trouble," Sana told gathering courage. "You come with us."

The victim girl walked on Sana's side.

"Let go, girls," Piyali said in a heroic tone.

"Wait, wait. How dare you? Don't you know how to communicate with your seniors?" one fellow said stepping towards them.

"Who are you to lecture in such a way?" the second guy responded.

"Which year?" the third boy asked.

Sana was now afraid but Piyali could see fear even in the group. She was an expert in catching the weak point of people.

"2nd year," Piyali said, turning her back to walk.

The group of boys kept watching. They did not mistreat them anymore because they knew to oppress a second-year student would let them face consequences.

"I have never seen her before," the fourth guy expressed in a thoughtful fashion.

"Leave it guys. We will see it later. Let's go," the group disappeared.

In the meantime, Sana, Piyali and the victim girl were in the auto heading towards the hostel. They did not wait for the college bus.

"Thank you so much," the girl replied in a feared nature.

"It's ok. It feels good to help others," Piyali said.

"What's your name?" Sana asked.

"Kavita. I am from Shillong."

"That's great. We are also from the same place," hearing this Kavita felt better.

When you are in a new place and you find someone from your native place, it provides you with immense joy and the probability of becoming good friends is high. It shows courage and rescue from homesickness.

"Thank you so much for this support. You two are damn courageous," Kavita said.

Piyali smiled.

The best-enjoyed smile is when you support someone and the person praise you from the core of her heart. The people who have experienced such a feeling can feel it.

"What the guys were telling you?" Sana asked.

"Those bastards have got a filthy mind. How can they tell such words?" Kavita said. "Someone from the back also said he would love it if I go down to him and…."

"Don't take it in mind," Piyali said. "Forget whatever happened."

"We will spend a good time from now," Sana said. "But Piyali, how did you say you are a second-year student?"

"When I spoke I saw one guy was murmuring in the back and was saying something like which year student I was. Their power is limited to first-year students only. So I applied the trick."

"What if they come to know you are not in the second year?" Kavita asked.

"We will face together," Piyali said.

"I do not want you to be in trouble for me," Kavita said.

"Don't worry Kavita. Hence now we will be together. They always make victim when they see alone," Sana said.

They reached the hostel. They took Kavita to their room. They talked the almost half night and that night's discussion made them friends.

***

One year and a few months passed and days were passing pleasantly till the day when three of them agreed to party. They arranged drinks in their room and concluded that there should none other than them.

"Kavita no guys," Piyali said during their time of planning the company.

"I understand Piyali," she replied taking it in mind.

Since the mid of the second year, there was little conflict between Piyali and Kavita. In the last one and a half year, they have formed many good buddies and the companions they established were common among them as they constantly stuck together. They had gained a title in the college, 'lesbo group.'

Devraj was one of their friends who spent time with these three girls. Sana was simple, and she maintained her simplicity. A boy in a group of a girl really helps. They could enjoy their late night show as they have one protector by their side and Devraj never said no to their proposal for planning.

Devraj a gentleman of a final year found his likeness in one. He joined the group for Kavita but he became a good friend to three of them. Devraj cared for them and he was too caring. He had the habit that could impress people around him.

Kavita somewhat liked him since the time he came to their group. Kavita being an independent girl had a mobile phone and Devraj used to call her.

When the night arrived the three girls sat in their place and began their drinks with slow romantic Hindi music.

When Piyali said no guys, she means to remind Kavita that not even Devraj. There was a cold war between them for Devraj.

"This will be the most extraordinary time of our life," Sana added putting up the beer mug.

"Every moment is great," Kavita said and raised her cup. Piyali accompanied her.

The first sip reached their stomach, and the absorption began.

"Let's move together for a job," Piyali said. "Way of life is too difficult without you."

"Let's sit for the same company," Sana said. "We will tell them if they want to enroll, they should select three of us and if not then none of us."

"Rightly said," Kavita told. "You speak great words darling, ummm…" she kissed Sana on her chick.

The alcohol was slowly crossing the blood-brain barrier and the effect started with Kavita.

"We will enjoy everything together," Piyali said in a hazy tone and she laughed.

"Piyali you quit speaking to Devraj," Kavita said.

"He is damn hot," Piyali said laughing. "I cannot avoid communicating to him."

"Why can't you find someone else? You always stick around him and I hate you for this," Kavita said.

"He is not your property," Piyali said. "He has never expressed his interest for you either."

Something was not right. They knew it was the drink that making them to talk rubbish.

"Please don't talk rubbish and ruin the night," Sana said trying to stop their arguing.

"I will propose him soon," Kavita said.

"He is not getting in a relationship now and he is really uffff," Piyali said and lay down on the floor."

"You are such a fool bitch," Kavita said.

"What did you say?" Piyali stood with her shaky legs and asked.

Now the conversation was getting really worse and such words really doubles the effect of the alcohol.

"You are even a big bitch. I see you hang around with that junior guy. How many you want at a time. Look at you first," Piyali said in a louder voice.

"You be away from my life and don't talk to Devraj," she said.

"I don't give a sheet to your words," Piyali stood kicking the glass on the floor. She went back to her bed. The glass broke. The beer spread in the room.

"Don't be a child," Sana said. "Enough, never ever we will organize such parties. Stupid you girls are," Sana said.

Kavita moved to her room and closed her door speaking to herself.

Sana remained seated on the floor trying to remove the broken pieces of the glass with her shaky hands.

CHAPTER THREE

Late in August Sana could grab an offer of a job she was searching. She had been idle for two months in quest of the post she always wanted. It was not just an offer to grip, but there were many rounds of interviews she had to make through to get the position, she got to know how competitive the world had become.

Just after concluding her final year of BSc she had relocated to the state of Karnataka to be more definite Bangalore. The planning she had made with Kavita and Piyali did not work out. Piyali's family did not grant her permission to go to a different state for a job. Kavita got selected before Sana, so she had moved two months earlier than Sana. Two months later, Sana was there.

"You don't have to worry about me," Sana had announced to her mom before leaving her home for this position.

She had invariably been an ideal person in all form of the character she played as of a daughter, a student, a human being, an Indian. Being an inhabitant of a small place of Meghalaya to be specific Shillong, she did not have many options for the future prosperity of her life.

Since the point she had taken up BSc, she had always wanted to work for an organization where she could take advantage of her knowledge. She had looked around her hometown, there was no other opportunity she had seen besides teaching, but it was not her favorite profession. So she had decided to shift in search of a career that could raise her in a short time.

Sana was the only child in the family; therefore, she was special to her parents. She had developed her maturity to grasp the situation early in her life to be more explicit since her class five. It was not an easy task for her parents to make, nevertheless, they let her shift to Bangalore, a place 3000 km away from her home.

"Let's move out elsewhere," Kavita called out.

"Kavita, I am not in the mood today," Sana said.

Since the ragging incident in first year Kavita, Sana and Piyali had become best friends. They had enjoyed their college to the utmost. It was in their college days that they first tasted alcohol, something they only used to see in the movies that they used to go.

"Why are you not interested on boyfriends?" Kavita asked, lying on her bed.

There were two small beds, each could accommodate one person. The bed was small such that even the hand of another person could not fit in it when the owner is lying on it.

"What should I answer to your inquiry?" Sana spoke, resting on her bed with the pillow on her lap. "I don't know why everyone worries so often about me because I am single. Have I committed any mistake by not being in relationship at this age?"

"Don't get irritated. I just asked," Kavita said.

Kavita knew Sana from college days, but they had been away from last few months as Kavita had moved to Bangalore for a career before Sana. Kavita always wanted Sana to join her as life for her was boring without her because she knew at that stage of life it's very difficult to find a friend whom she could trust like Sana or Piyali.

You always remain in a concern you cannot get another friend whom you can trust and enjoy with more than your school or childhood friends.

The expression on Kavita's face made a change in the mood of Sana, and she smiled looking at her and said smirking, "I do not want to repeat the same incident that happened between you and Piyali. No boyfriend, no talks, and no quarrel."

Kavita laughed, and the images of that night were alive again in her. "We were so dumb in those days. How could we fight on that nonsense topic?"

"Leave it apart. I think someone from here will propose you soon or later," Kavita said. "Enough of remaining single."

Sana laughed at her. "Time is over baby. That craziness is over now, and now it's all about parents and let the fortune decide what it wants to."

It is true that the insanity that excites you in your school and college days slowly perishes as you mature. It may happen that you began liking someone, but you cannot just madly fall for the person. The minds become too choosy to choose the right person.

"Yeah, I agree with you partly," Kavita said. She was about to say something more when she was interrupted.

"Now tell me about your boyfriends?" Sana asked.

The appearance of Kavita had changed and she seemed to be the type of a girl with line of boyfriends. She had few boyfriends in the past, and she had ditched most of them. Situations had forced her to ditch the boyfriends hence we cannot make any judgment.

"First of all, I have a boyfriend, and not boyfriends," she said. "You know how much I love Devraj."

"This is what I like about you so much. You are always into Devraj, and it's really good. Girls these days take advantage of having a disproportionate ratio of girls and boys in our country. As the number of boys is more, many acquire a few of them," Sana said like a guardian.

"Thank you."

"You are lucky to have Devraj," Sana said.

"Luck will knock your doors too," Kavita said. "It knocks everyone's door, and even if you don't open the door, it comes back in other form and knocks again, but it comes."

"Cool philosophy," Sana said, smiling.

"It's true," Kavita said. "You are too beautiful to remain single."

Sana smiled but remained silent, staring at Kavita. She was indeed a pretty young woman. She had long brown hair. Brown not by birth but she maintained it brown, and her hair seems adopted the color and produced a natural look. Her thin eyebrow and big eyeballs gave her a true look. Her height creates jealousy in many of the surrounding girls. Her look gave none clue understanding which state she belonged.

"And that is why I am waiting to get a knock on my door in the other best form," Sana said and laughed.

They were doing nothing rather than the useless talk but indeed if it was of no use, there was nothing they could do at that moment as they had just arrived from work.

"It's too late, we need to cook," Kavita said peering at her mobile.

"It's 9, and you know it's time for my Arzu," Sana said. Sana stood from her bed and switched on TV.

Sana was an addict of a TV series 'Ishq me tere' where the main character of the story was Arzu Siddiqui. She was a great fan of him. She even celebrated his birthday. She used to cut the cake on his birthday. Every 2nd January she celebrated his birthday. Since her first year of college, she had been addicted to this series.

'Ishq me Tere' gained its popularity quickly. There were thousands to lakhs of fans for this series. The story of the sequence goes like this:

Arzu and Sara are childhood friends. They have completed their school, and college together. Till school, they were great buddies and there was a desire for each other, but being so good friend neither of them could convey. When they got into college Arzu gathered the courage to reveal his feeling for her.

Sara Happily accepted the proposal, and they enjoyed another phase of life.

There were no bumps in their path. Both their families were happy. In fact, it made them delightful to know finally; they decided to be together for their entire life.

Family background of Sara was economically less developed, but it did not impact their relationship.

After completion of their college, Arzu moves to a renowned university of Canada for his further study and Sara joined a private company in her hometown.

Because of not well-developed technology during those days the point of contact for Arzu and Sara remained limited to landline calls, costing a huge amount, especially for international calls.

In the meantime, Sara falls for another guy in her workplace. She refrains it from Arzu, but her conscience knew she was doing wrong. She never wanted to fall for anyone rather than Arzu, but she could not believe her feelings. She did not understand how talking to a guy regularly led her fall for him irrespective of being in a relationship.

One year thereafter, when Arzu comes back home he becomes overwhelmed by the news. It brings tears in his eyes. No, it was not the story of Sara's other relationship. It was the news of Sara's health. She was diagnosed with knee cancer and because of this; her new relationship had ended up two months before the arrival of Arzu. She had informed nothing about her weakness towards that new guy.

Arzu moves from one hospital to another taking her, and struggling to find the best possible treatment as he was aware Sara's parents could never afford her treatment. He loved her so extreme, and he invariably had felt that he could not survive without her.

The tears in his minds and deteriorating condition of Arzu forced Sara to let Arzu know everything about her as the guilt in her was tearing her bit by bit. She informed him all about her fragility towards the guy in her office.

The last episode that Sana was watching was the scene when the leg of Sara was cut out to save her life.

The story was so framed that it made people addicted to people who liked love stories.

"That's the end. Now let's go. We need to cook," Kavita replied and stepped to switch off the TV.

"I want to know the whole story. I can't wait. It's making me crazy," she added. "Do you think Arzu will continue to love her the same way? She is so bitching. How can she cheat the guy who loved her so much?"

You always try to find mistakes of the people who try to remain close to the person whom you like so much just to ditch your anger and get a chance to give your anger a form and that is why Sara becomes a bitch in the eyes of Sana.

"You are so much into it," Kavita replied, walking to the kitchen. "It's scripted, and not a true story. Let the story flow according to the writer, and don't give your inputs. Now come, and help me cut the cabbage."

"Life is so much full of work," Sana said, as she stood from her bed walking to the kitchen to look for anything available that they would cook for dinner.

"Don't worry, I will search for you a guy who will do these house works as you watch your Arzu day and night," Kavita said, as she walked to the kitchen.

"Looking for a non-working husband with experience in housework should be my status from today," she responded both laughed out loud.

CHAPTER FOUR

"Hey, can you do a little favor for me?" a person not well known by Sana asked sitting opposite to her.

Sana was at her assigned place in the organization and was working. Her responsibility as a new employee was data entry. The floor of the company was lined with rows of the desktop with a central control unit, and in every row, there were about 92 desktops. The working area of each member was covered with a glass slab making partial visibility of the work each member carried out. Each person had their own area. She turned back on hearing someone talking to her.

She looked at the guy, and could summon she had met him during the training days but had not interacted, thus, she could not recall his name. It is too difficult for some people to remember the names of new faces.

"Go ahead," she answered, and continued with her job.

"I need a little support in my work. I cannot process this document, and it is not even clear," the person said. "You need to have a look at my desktop."

Sana remained seated on her chair and something filled her with confidence. Being a new employee, she was asked to help another new employee, and she felt happy, but she did not express her happiness. She stood from her chair stepped to look at the document. A notepad with a pen was kept near the keyboard. She pushed the notepad and could see the name on the notepad as Rudra.

"You cannot process this document. You see this," Sana said, pointing with her finger. "Half of it is not visible. Report it to your concerned person."

"Thank you, Sana," the guy replied with a smile.

Some guys are really so positive about life. They are so positive that even if the girl of their like looks at them once, they deep in the ocean of thoughts.

Sana came back to her desk. She looked at Kavita, who at this time was smiling looking at her. Kavita raised a hand to thump up, and expressed the best luck.

Sana hid her smile and continued her work.

Rudra was the candidate who was trained with the batch of Sana. There were ten new candidates, but Sana hardly interacted with anyone. She remained busy with her friend Kavita. She had always remained fixed with the suggestion of her friends because she knew friendship in the later part of life is based on the way you can be useful to the person, and not just for the interest of friendship.

A few minutes later, Kavita came to Sana, and sat beside her pulling a chair by her side.

"Things are going right," she said, putting her hand on her shoulder.

"You are too much into it," I think you are already into him. "I have been watching you since the time of training how you kept looking at him," Sana said.

"Is it an offense to look at someone the way you mean? You know well how much I am into my Devraj," Kavita said.

"Looking is not an offense but staring is," she said looking at her face.

"Oh I see, jealous," Kavita said smiling.

"I do not understand why you think so. I don't even look at him," Sana said as she continued with her typing.

"Just see how he is attractive. He has good physic too; tall, dark, and handsome. He has all the quality you need," Kavita said.

"Now complete your work. I don't prefer to talk about this matter anymore," Sana said pushing her.

Kavita stood, and whispered to her ear, "He can lift you." She said with a naughty tone, and walked away.

Sana did not bother about the words of Kavita. She forgot in a while and remained dipped in her own work.

***

Sana was on her bed lost in some thoughts from her past. Loneliness makes past alive, and sometimes it feels great to give life to your prior experiences. Her earphone was plugged in her ear, and her eyes were closed listening to the same sets of songs again and again from her iPod. Favorite music, and memories are the finest combinations a person can enjoy at its best. Kavita interrupted her thought process.

"Piyali," she said, handing the phone to her.

Piyali had called up in Kavita's mobile. She often called, and talked to them. She could not make it to be away from her home because of the restriction imposed by her parents. But she always remained in touch through calls.

Piyali's family was orthodox, and did not feel it good to send their daughter away from home for a job. They were still in the old era where they believed women were meant only to be housewives. There were many obstacles in her education, but with the support of her two friends and dedication, she could complete her education.

"Hey miss busy," Piyali responded, with excitement. "It's been so long you haven't called me up."

Piyali, Sana and Kavita were the groups of friends who shared almost everything and every moment of their lives since their college days. They had a very strong bonding. They were always together even during their job, but only Sana and Kavita could make it remain close.

"Hey, stud addicted," Sana replied. "How come you thought about me today?"

"You can forget me because you have new friends and a new place to enjoy but I can't do," Piyali said.

"If you had new friends, you would have forgotten me, that's what I can conclude from your words," Sana said, turning to another side.

"Shut up. I have never won an argument with you. So I raise my hand," Piyali said with a smile in her face. "I miss both of you so much."

"We always miss you. There is always something empty between us, and that was only you who used to fill it," Sana replied in a heavy tone.

It is tough to be away from your friends with whom you have spent all your childhood and college.

"I do not want to make us sad anymore. I have called to inform you about my engagement," Piyali said.

"Whoa, whoa… I can't believe what you are saying. How…I mean when," Sana said, getting up from her bed in excitement. "You have never told us anything like this before. How long was this process going on? How could you hide it from us?"

"It's a long story. I will tell you once you get here for the bachelor party," Piyali said, and kept shut.

She knew hundreds of questions would come now, and she had to deal with. She tried her best to describe everything after meeting as discussing things with friends in a real meeting gives so much fun. But she was also ready to respond to all the questions, however, she kept the secrets to reveal when they come to the party.

"Kavita why aren't you talking?" she asked before Sana asked her anything. "I will not talk about Devraj."

As the phone was in loudspeaker mode, Kavita could hear her.

"You are still in the same place," Kavita said. "Now it does not matter even if you take him."

The weird incident of that midnight in college always made them laugh. They had wanted that night to become memorable, and it had turned into being a memorable one. They might have forgotten about it had that incident not occurred. Sometimes bad incidents help in a hasty manner.

"Ha ha ha… Now that the fragrance of the originality has gone, you want to throw it on me," Piyali said.

"Same face, same voice, same talks every day," Kavita said, and smiled.

"Jokes apart, plan to come," Piyali said.

"First tell me everything about him, and how far have you gone. When did it happen?" Sana asked. She was still at her excitement to listen to the sudden decision of her friend.

"It was my fortune. I never thought I will get married to the right person of my choice, but fortunately the boy chosen by my family turned out to be our friend," Piyali said. "Do you remember the candy boy of our class who left college at the end of the first year?"

"Ummm…Wait I think I know," Sana tried her best to recall, and then asked for some clue.

"Long hair, used to be shy talking to girls but girls would talk about him," Piyali said.

"Oh… I got it... OMG...You are going to eat that little chocolate baby," Sana said recalling the boy.

Kavita's mouth remained wide open knowing that Piyali was getting engaged to the chocolate boy, as if it was practically impossible for any girl to get him.

"Don't talk rubbish," Piyali said, blushing.

"You used to be a chocolate lover, and finally the chocolate came to you. Don't bite him hard," Sana said, laughing loud.

"I am not as strong as you. I will try my best, but I know my bite force would be hundred times less than that you wanted to give to that guy," Piyali said. "Do you remember?"

"I used to just kid around, but you have bought yourself to that position," Sana said.

"Stop this rubbish stuff now," Piyali said. "Without you, everything will be remaining undecided. Decide along with Kavita, and let me know which date you are free in the next month."

"Yeah, baby. We will never miss this opportunity. I will notify you after discussing."

"Sure," Piyali said, and hang up.

Sana was thrilled, and excited about the news. She wanted to leave everything behind, and run to her friend and enjoy every moment with her. She wanted to have a lot of fun, and all the decision they had made during the college days to attend the engagements of each other wherever they are. And now she realized how time passed promptly, and they were in the period they had discussed decades ago.

She waited with all the amazing news jumping within her to be spread out. She jumped to hug Kavita.

"Enough Sana," Kavita said. "I think Piyali is not so much happy as you are now."

"I don't know why my excitement raise so much. I can't wait to see the day," Sana said, and loosened Kavita.

"Do you think we can attend?" Kavita asked. "You know well how limited holidays we have."

"I will resign if I don't get the leave," she said.

"Yes, we can do that, I agree to do the same," she supported her.

"She made an ideal decision, luck also sided with her," Kavita said, adding. "The chocolate of our class. But why at an immediate?" she said and, came close to Sana. "Is she pregnant?"

This is the most symbolic call of the Indian folk when someone gets married without proper pre-planning.

"Maybe," Sana said, and both chuckled loud

CHAPTER FIVE

"Don't change this song," Sana screamed to the person who was going down towards the music system.

Everyone was dancing to the beat of the music, and no one bothered about the steps they were performing. There were around thirty people dancing on the floor. Before the start of the party, Piyali had opened all to everyone, so it became easy for everyone to adapt to the new environment with the new faces.

It was a small bachelor party thrown by Piyali, just two days before her engagement, and it was at the request of her friends she had to arrange for the bachelor party. Including all her friends and her cousins, the number reached thirty.

Sana and Kavita had arrived just the night before, and they had arranged everything for the party. They were more like family members than just friends.

Though Sana shouted at highest of her voice, no one bothered, and the person who was pacing forward to change the song stopped at that spot, and danced again.

"I am so happy that you all have come," Piyali said, loudly decreasing the volume of the music, and raising her glass of beer.

"We had waited for this day for so long," Kavita shouted to her highest voice with her mis-balance body almost falling on Sana.

They were not regular drinkers. They hardly opt for drinks, but as it was the day for their best friend, they could not deny.

Sana was dancing. She was enjoying every move of her dance and emotion gradually was taking over her. She held Piyali dancing, and suddenly she broke into her arms saying, "I will miss you so much. You are everything to me. Don't go away, please."

She was all on Piyali. Piyali sat keeping her on her lap. Slowly Sana's eyes closed. Kavita ran to her. Looking at her face she said, "Sleep."

Kavita tried to wake her, but she was out of her sleep world too. She could only be awakened when the shelf life of alcohol was over. Few of her friends, and other participants also gathered around.

"Let me help you Piyali," Samar said, coming forward.

Samar was a friend of Piyali not common to Kavita and Sana. Samar helped Piyali to lift Sana, and take her to the bedroom. And this scene was enough to end the bachelor's party that night. Bachelor's party was a crime according to Piyali's parents, so to keep things from complication they ended the party.

"She is so innocent," Samar said to Piyali while leaving the room.

"Yeah because she is my friend," Piyali said.

"By the way, I got one more friend with the same name. Are you related?" Piyali asked walking towards Samar.

"You are dumb. Should everyone with the same name be related?" Samar asked, laughing at the naïve question of Piyali.

"I thought it might be as you both are common friends of mine. The only difference is that I am rarely in touch with Samar," she said. "Had he come in this party I would have introduced you."

"I am not interested in a man," he said. "I am interested in a woman. Would you please introduce me to your friend Sana?"

Piyali smiled and said, "I could do it but now she is out. I will discuss with her tomorrow, and will let you know about her decision."

"Thanks," he said and walked away. Everyone left.

***

Sana woke up from her heavy sleep. For a moment, she remained lost to remember where she was. She had practically forgotten the party of the last night. She rubbed her eyes trying to open it wide. She found the room empty, and slowly she could think of the place. She walked down from the bed, and stepped out of the door. She could see everyone was busy doing something. Looking at her, Piyali came running, "Hey."

"Why was I still sleeping?" she asked.

"hahahaahahah…..," Piyali laughed, closing her mouth with her hand. "I don't understand what to tell you. You drank so much yesterday."

"Oh… I think I had spoilt the party. I am so sorry," Sana said.

Piyali was nevertheless, continuing with her laugh.

"Get ready. We have a lot of work to do," Piyali said.

Piyali being the only child of her parents took all responsibility. It was her own engagement, but she handled everything with the help of her friends, and Sana was one of those friends to handle the responsibilities.

Sana tried to smile looking at the laughing face of Piyali, and stepped in the room. She was still confused and wanted to recall about the last night but her brain failed to bring back the happening.

In the evening Piyali, Sana and Kavita sat discussing the requirement for the engagement day. Piyali brought the topic of Samar.

"Besides all the important things to discuss, it is important to discuss Samar's interest on you," Piyali said pointing Sana.

Now all the eyes were on Sana. It was as if Sana had told Samar to show his interest in her. Though it made her feel good, she did not let her face express it.

Samar was really a cool guy. His personality matched the favorite character of Sana from her favorite tv serial 'Ishq me tere.' Samar resembled Arzu and in the eyes of Sana, he was totally Arzu. Sana was so mad for Arzu that she would accept Samar's proposal at any instance of time. When Piyali had introduced him in the last afternoon, she had looked deep into him. She had stolen many glances bringing her favorite character to live looking at him.

"No, I am not interested," she said usually, smiling inside.

"I have seen you watching him during the party," Kavita said. "You have spent most of your time getting a glance of him."

"How do you know that I was watching him," Sana resisted.

"He is the one in whom many girls see their favorite character," Piyali said.

Sana smiled, and this smile was enough to show her interest in Samar. She wanted that some magic should happen so she could be with him.

"If you had a mobile, I could have shared your number with him," Piyali said.

"You can better give Samar's number to Sana. We will see how to progress," Kavita said, and winked to Sana.

Piyali opened the contact list of her mobile. She wrote the number on a piece of paper, and handed over to Sana.

"Why don't you call him with your number, and talk now," Kavita asked Piyali.

"You are right. Good presence of mind," she said and dialed the number, but the number was out of reach.

"No, bad luck," she said, making a face. "Out of reach."

"Nothing bad luck. The entire day he has spent here, and so his battery is dead, I think," Kavita said, against Piyali.

"You can call him next day," Piyali said, and they started their usual gossip.

***

Days passed, but Sana did not call up the number Piyali gave. She was afraid to call. She did not know what she should say after calling him. Will he agree to talk to her? So many fears filled in her, and pulled her from calling him. But a final day came when she gathered some courage, went to the nearby PCO of her work location, and dialed the number. She could have used Kavita's mobile, but she knew how Kavita remains attached with her phone talking to Devraj. She hardly maintained balance as every time Devraj used to call her. So Sana had decided to use the coin booth. The main reason behind not using Kavita's mobile was a past issue which had hurt Sana so much that she had promised herself that she would never use Kavita's mobile for her own purpose.

Fortunately, she could hear the ringing.

"Hi," she said, as Samar received the call.

"Who is this?" Samar asked.

She waited for a while. She could not understand what to say. She knew that even if she told him her name, he might not recognize her. She thought to check if he remembered her name.

"We met in the party last week," she said. "Do you remember?"

"I have not been to a party since a month," he replied.

What is he talking? Has he really forgotten everything? Had he seen me after he was out by his drink? Did Piyali lie to me that he was interested in me? Many thoughts passed by her mind. For a while she was afraid that she had made call to some wrong number.

"Are you not Samar?" she asked.

"Yeah I am Samar," the reply came.

"What is your name?" Samar asked.

"Are you sure you don't remember anything about the bachelor party of Piyali's engagement?"

"I was busy so I could not come," he said.

"So you are a friend of Piyali," he said. "Where do you stay?"

"Currently staying in Bangalore," she said.

No sooner did she say this than he was excited.

He was very happy. He felt to jump with joy. He had asked about her many times, but Piyali had not even revealed her name to him. She did just inform him that she works in Bangalore. A true friend will always maintain your privacy until he/she get a confirmation.

"No, I can't believe how you can forget things completely," Sana said

"I wish I would be there at the party," he said.

Sana smiled and still, she was not sure about the matter that he has forgotten the incidence.

"All right I assume that you were not there," she said.

"How did you get my contact number," he asked smiling within. It was as if his dream came true. He always had the desired to go ahead with the proposal of friendship, but he did not get the chance to go ahead. But today luck has itself walked to him.

"I thought you had something to talk to me on that day," she said again reminding him of the party.

"I wish I had been there at the party," he said. He was still confused about the fact she was talking. "Is this your contact number?"

Can alcohol erase some memory completely?

"I don't use a mobile," she said. "I am calling you from a coin booth."

Coin booths during those days were very popular. A one rupee coin would let you talk for 60 seconds and before the 60-second ends you have to feed another coin and the process goes on till you complete your conversation. She had already fed ten coins, and was at the eleventh.

"Huh!!! How is it possible?" he said in surprise. "I mean how a person could survive without a phone, and even when you are so far from home."

"But I am surviving," she said.

"I am sorry. I have already spent a lot of your coins," he said expressing sorry.

"It's fine," she said, searching for another coin in her handbag.

"Tomorrow you call me at the same time. I will call you back in the same number," he said.

A feeling of caring nature of the person from the other end of the phone hit her, and it brought a bright smile on her. She smiled and placed back the receiver politely.

Love makes people polite.

She walked back to her room. Her jolly face was enough to reveal to Kavita that she had successfully talked to Samar.

"Oh look at you, how you are smiling within," Kavita said, as Sana walked to the room.

"Nothing that sort of happened," she said throwing her handbag on her bed, and lifting the water bottle from the table.

"Just one phone call and your thirst are at its peak," Kavita said in a tone.

"Shut up," Sana said. "You are so negative."

"Let me know something about your discussion," Kavita asked, coming near to her.

Both sat on her bed, and Sana said, "He is a sort of short-term memory person."

"Why? What's wrong with him?"

"He has forgotten almost everything about the party. He doesn't even remember that he had attended the party," Sana said, walking to and fro in the room.

"You are so innocent," Kavita said. "He is just checking on you. He is trying to know your interest for him. And you know that might have given him a pleasure to know that the girl he has expressed his desire for is into so much to talk to him."

"I don't understand what is going on," Sana said.

"Don't worry. It's just the beginning," Kavita said.

CHAPTER SIX

"Hey, is everything all right?" Samar asked.

It was the day four of their conversation, and now the duration of their conversation had gone far more. Every day at 4 in the evening, Sana used to go to the coin booth, and spent her next 45 minutes there. Now she did not have to carry one rupee coins. She used to call him with her first coin and Samar would call back to the same number.

"Yeah, feeling better to know that I am getting to know more about the person I like these days," she said, smiling.

"That's new input to your brain," Samar said, smiling back. "But I have already started knowing you much before."

"Yeah, I can see it. You know about me so much that you don't even know my name," Sana said. "And you don't remember that we met at the party."

"I wish I had met you in the party," Samar said. He repeated the same answer whenever Sana asked him about the bachelor party that she claim it is where she met him.

Two questions always kept both of them in thought. Sana always thought how someone could completely erase the memory of one day of his life? She assumed that it might happen due to over drinking, but she expected that he would recall in the next day or maybe later, but it wasn't happening. She justified it with her own situation of that day. She could recall that she had also forgotten the incidence when she became out in that night.

Samar remained lost in the thought when he did meet her. He could recall that he did not go to the party. He did not investigate the matter further and framed the answer, "I wish I had."

"Knowing you is not a difficult task as you know I am well connected with Piyali, but I want to know you personally not with any third-party information. It gives me excitement to know you more. The incomplete information always creates a demand," Samar said.

Sana remained silent for a few seconds, took a deep breath, and replied, "Hmmm… Which place do you come from exactly?"

"Somewhere in Shillong," he replied.

"I know it, but where is this 'somewhere' in Shillong?" She asked.

"Maybe few miles from your locality," he said.

Sana could understand that there was something he did not want to reveal about his location. She knew Samar belongs to Shillong and even Samar knew that Sana belongs from Shillong, but Shillong is not just place with few people.

"Tell me about the place you're now talking from," Samar asked.

"The coin booth is stuck to the corner of the shop. At the entry, the owner sits with a table and a few files. The other side of the room is occupied with the PCO where there is always a rush. The owner is really a good person. He has never told me anything about taking so long time. Just on the opposite to the road that runs in between is a cd shop where hundreds of cd hang best of Kumar Sanu, best of Zubeen and many more," she said explaining the complete scenario of the place.

"You explain things too good," he said.

She did not reply but smiled.

"Till I know your real name, I should give you a name," he said. He always made her feel special. He knew how she could be happy. His words were touching her.

"I would love to carry the name on me, you give," she said.

"Look at the cd shop once again," he said.

"Why?" she asked in confusion.

Suddenly her heartbeat rose. She thought Samar might have come there and he wanted to give her a surprise. She liked Samar because he resembled her favorite tv character, but she was not ready to meet him that early. She had decided to know him completely before meeting him. She removed the receiver from her ear and turned to look at the cd shop. She could see two guys standing near the shop. She could not see their faces.

"Tell me one actress name that you can see on the cd," he asked.

She inhaled long and breathed in peace. 'Thank god,' she said to herself.

"Is it not visible?" he asked, getting no response.

"It's visible. I can see Riya sen's pic clearly," she said. "But why?"

"So your name for me is Riya." Is it ok?"

She thought for a while and smiled. She liked the name. You compare a girl with a beautiful actor; by her expression, it may appear it does not matter, but deep down she must be very happy.

"When you have already decided, how can I say no," she said.

***

Two months had passed. Sana and Samar enjoyed the regular conversation. Sana had asked many times to meet once before the relation takes a real shape, but Samar always made an excuse to avoid the planning for a meet.

"I do not know what is happening to me. He is so much into me these days. I have not talked to him face to face. I want to meet him before I go too far. His words are so addictive. I asked him once to meet, and he said very soon we would meet, but I do not know the word 'soon' contains how many hours, days, months or years," Sana said with a different voice.

The word soon is really confusing. No one knows what the exact meaning of the word. Sana wished such word should not have existed.

"Why are you getting impatient," Kavita said, coming near to her, keeping her phone aside. She put her hand on her shoulder. "It is just the beginning, and it goes this way. He will meet you. Let him also fall deeply for you, and he will be made to meet with you."

"It was his interest to talk to me. He even has shown his interest for me and expressed to Piyali, but he is not clear when he is going to meet me," Sana said. "It does not happen this way."

Sana had seen how crazy boys go for meeting their girls, especially in the days of the beginning of their relationship. Even

Kavita had told her how Devraj used to find a way just to meet her. She felt that something was not right.

"You are expecting things too quickly. Just remember everything has its prescribed time. You know Samar is the guy whom many girls want in their life. When a person is in such demand, he will have some attitude, but it is nothing to worry about," Kavita tried to make Sana understand with an artificial smile.

She was also in doubt about the ignorance of Samar to meet. Though they knew Samar was somewhere far, they expected that he should have been crazy to meet her.

Sana suddenly turned to Kavita and looking at her face said, "Should I continue to talk to him the same way?"

Kavita could not think of what to answer. She knew how serious Sana becomes with the thing she is attached. She had to give an answer that neither should depress Sana nor should affect her life in the future.

"I would suggest you give some time. If you feel like something is wrong happening, you can quit. It's just the phone calls now," Kavita said.

Sana remained silent and began to think for a while.

"It's 9, let's go," Kavia said and switched on the tv, and the faimilar romantic music started to play.

At the episode, Arzu Siddiqui appeared in the opening scene and seeing him Sana's eyes filled with tears.

She closed her eyes and stood. She left to watch, and it was perhaps the first day that Sana ignored the show. His face, his voice reminded her of Samar.

She went back to her bed and laid down. She dipped her face in the pillow and remained silent. Kavita came rolling her hand on her back and said, "Stop thinking negative. He has not ditched you. What makes you think so negative?"

"I do not know what is happening to me," she said and wiped her tears.

Kavita did not know what she should do to calm her.

"Don't be too much into it. Food is more important," she said to bring smile in Sana's face. "Today we will cook a new dish," Kavita held her hand to pull her to the kitchen. She knew making her busy with something would give her some comfort.

They had their dinner and again came to bed. Kavita wanted to listen to some music, so she switched on TV and tuned to a music channel.

"I can't believe this," Sana said in surprise. She was standing with Samar but Samar now entirely looked like Arzu, and they were in the center of the hall of a royal palace. Not only Samar looked like Arzu, but also, he has taken up the profession of acting. She looked, and thought Samar and Arzu are the same person and he had kept it back from her just to give her a big surprise. The palace was so perfect that Sana could not believe it was a real palace made with some precious stones and not an artificial one. She ran all around the palace, and there were many people working; some were busy decorating each and every corner of the palace, some people were busy cleaning. The palace itself seemed to be an industry where hundreds of people were employed.

"I have always dreamt of you," Sana said, coming closer to

Samar and hugged him. She touched his face and tried to feel it. I have watched every episode. Since the days I started watching 'Ishq me tere' I was in love with you."

"I was waiting all these days for you," Samar replied. "I knew one day someone like you would come who would complete be my other half, and you really completed me today."

"All these days I have seen you only in the screen, and today I am with you. I do not know how I came here," she could not believe her destiny. "Why I am here? Did you call me? Did you want me here?"

"Look all around," Samar said, holding her shoulder and pointing all the decorations and the ongoing works. "These people are working because in the next half an hour the next episode of your favorite series will be shooting here."

"Wha...wha...what, do you mean I am going watch your serial live now?" she said with an unbelievable thought.

"Yeah, just watch it," Samar said and began to walk towards the crowd.

As Samar started to walk, Sana wanted to walk behind him, but she could not move. She tried again, but in vain. She tried to call out his name, but she was volume less. She could see slowly Samar mixed with the crowd, and did not turn to see Sana. Sana kept on trying to run, and shout, but she could not move and suddenly her eyes opened.

She could see Kavita was asleep, and the tv was still on. She looked all around, and finally came to reality from her dream world. She had fallen for Samar not for what Samar is, but because Samar looks like Arzu, and she was mad for Arzu. She switched off the tv, smiled wide thinking about the dream and laid down on her bed.

Sometime dreams give you something which you may or may not achieve in life, but for the moment it takes you to your desired world with the desired happening around you. Some says dream is the composition of thoughts both from your conscious and subconscious brain.

CHAPTER SEVEN

"Now you must be happy. Now that you have got your mobile, it does not mean you will avoid talking to me," Kavita said, handing over the mobile to Sana.

Sana and Kavita had come to the market to buy a mobile. A mobile in those days meant so much. Not every person could afford to make calls with mobiles. Back then he mobile which cost 3k now would cost eight hundred only. As it was Sunday, their evening was packed with, planning to shop, roam around, and eat street food and so on.

"I should make my first call to him," Sana said and inserted the sim that she had purchased a week ago.

She dialed the number and Samar received the call. They started talking. The most awkward moment is when you move out with a friend, and your friend becomes busy with her phone.

"Walk fast, we need to attend the party," Kavita said.

"I don't like parties at all," Sana said.

Kavita burst out in laughing, saying, "It has not just begun, and restriction started."

"No, Samar has not said anything, it's my wish," Sana said. "Do you think I am someone to be controlled by someone else?"

"I did not think of it all these days but from now, I think I should," Kavita said.

"There is nothing like that," Sana said.

"Walk fast, we need to attend the party," Kavita said.

It was a small success party thrown by their company for the achievement of that month though they did not have much input. Kavita wanted to attend the party at any cost because she believed making a good connection with people would help her to uplift in her job life and the party was vital for such opportunities.

"It's too late. We need to go back and get ready for the party," Sana said. "We can't dress in our best at this short time."

"Samar won't come to the party," Kavita said laughing.

"Do you dress only for Devraj?" Sana asked. Whenever she did something, Kavita always brought up the name of Samar.

"Yeah, of course. Whenever Devraj informs me that he is about to come, I become ready for him. I prepare myself at my best to impress him more," Kavita said, looking at Sana.

"I see your make up even when we go for office," Sana said. "I do not which Devraj comes to office everyday."

Talking to each other, they reached their room. They dressed as quick as possible and finally were at the party.

The party had begun before their arrival. They directly join the dance floor.

"You are late," the manager said, dancing and coming to them.

"We started early but traffic jam sir," Sana said. "And you know traffic in this city, especially in the evening."

The manager was amiable, he was not like other managers who would use girls to promote the business. He was a decent guy. He loved the employees' in the company.

"All right, enjoy," saying this, he stepped back to his team.

"Thank you, sir," Kavita shouted at her highest voice as the volume of the music was very high.

They could see everyone was taking sips and dancing.

"Should we?" Kavita asked Sana.

"Of course, it's party time," Sana moved and brought the drinks.

"But don't spoil it like the day in bachelor party," Kavita said.

They started dancing and consuming beer. Everyone was dancing. Many guys were staring at them.

"Hi," the same guy, Rudra who sits next to Sana and always ask for help from Sana.

"Hey," Sana replied.

"You are looking good," he said.

"Thanks," she said.

Kavita looked at them and smiled. She did not interfere in their conversation and she turned back, and danced accompanying the other person of their office.

Sana remained concerned with her dance and drink.

Slowly Sana was getting the hazy feeling. Alcohol was now being absorbed by the body, crossing her blood brain barrier. Slowly by slowly her movement stated changing; she could not support herself.

The guy was still dancing near to Sana. He looked at her and thought it was the perfect moment.

"Sana," he said coming close to her. "Will you go on a date with me?"

Sana laughed loudly closing her eyes. No one heard her laughter due to the high music volume.

"I don't understand what you are telling me," Sana said and this time she completed her glass.

"I want to go on a date with you," he whispered in her ear.

"Samar, you know," she said in a lazy tone. "He is dating me."

Kavita saw Rudra near Sana for long so she came there.

"What's going on?" she asked.

"Who is Samar?" he asked coming near to Kavita.

The music went on.

"Sana's dream boy," she said. "You can look for someone else. Or I can give you a better option."

"I would love to get your advice," the guy said.

"Find someone else. Don't waste your time on her," Kavita said.

"I like her form the first day I saw her," Rudra said.

"You like her, it does not mean she has to like you back. Like the people who likes you back," Kavita said.

"Let me talk to Sana regarding this," he said and was moving close to Sana.

"Listen, Kavita said. "Talk to her when alcohol effect is gone because whatever she is going to say now, she will forget by tomorrow. Alcohol has a bad effect on her memory."

"All right, help me to talk to her when she is out of this," he said. "Give me your number I will call you and you can help me to talk to her by today." He pulled out his mobile to save the number.

"Give me your mobile," Kavita said and snatched his mobile. She dialed her number and saved it. She handed over the phone to him.

Somehow Kavita was jealous that Rudra gave so much importance to Sana even though Sana never cared for it.

"Thanks," he said, and moved to his friends.

***

"Wake up, it's too late," Kavita said.

They had to get ready for their work, but the hangover of the last night for Sana was not over. She was still lying on her bed.

"What was that guy was saying yesterday at the party?" Sana asked, making a lazy, sleepy voice.

"We will talk about it later. Now get ready quickly," Kavita said.

"You are like my mom," Sana said and stepped down from her bed. She searched for her toothbrush.

They shared a common room, so they had to use the washroom planned way to save some time for sleeping.

"Be quick Kavita," Sana shouted with a mouthful of foam.

"Almost done," Kavita replied.

"I think Devraj is texting you, be quick I am not going to see it," Sana said.

Kavita came out of the bathroom and first checked her mobile. She found Rudra had texted asking about Sana. Kavita replied and kept her phone aside to get ready.

Within a short time, they were both ready, waiting for the bus which the company had provided.

"Rudra wanted to date you," Kavita said taking the next sit to Sana.

"What!!! How can he think so? You know boys are like this. You should not even help them. I don't know why he thinks like this," Sana said, stretching her explanation further. "Just because I help him in his office work, does it mean he should propose me? If this is so then, I would voluntarily stand in a public forum and ask all girls never to help a stranger."

"Don't overact Sana," Kavita said in a laughing tone. "You knew it very well why he used to come to you every day for help, and you sort of liked it."

"You are out of your mind," Sana said.

No one on the bus paid attention to their conversation as everyone in the bus were busy with their gossip.

"It's not a big issue that he asked for a date. It is a natural phenomenon. He is at least not like you. He told you he like you. Now you have Samar tell him you are in love"

"What do you mean not like me?" Sana asked, and her face turned red in anger.

"Why are you quarreling with that issue," Kavita said. "I have already told him that you are already in a relationship."

The bus arrived, and everyone got down and moved to their workplace. Sana did not look at anyone and walked straight to her assigned place. Rudra looked at her, but Sana did not. She sat and started working.

A little later, Rudra came again for help.

"I have my work to do," Sana refused to help him. "Try yourself. You can do it."

***

"Hey," Piyali said. "I have been calling you for like twenty-five minutes, but your phone was busy."

In the evening when they were in the room, Pyali had called.

"Sorry, I was talking to him," Sana said. "How are things going? How many nights already spent with your fiancée."

"I think what I have not done physically you have completed over the phone," Piyali said laughing.

"I was never that smart as you," Sana said, smiling looking at Kavita.

Kavita signaled to keep the phone on loudspeaker mode.

"Hearing a lot of things about you Piyali," Kavita said. "Keep something to enjoy after marriage."

"Keep your mouth shut. Don't talk like bitches," Piyali

shouted.

"Now that you're 'playing the game' dog and bitch, the words are getting stuck in your mouth," Sana said, both of them burst into laughter.

"By the way, yesterday Samar called me. He is too possessive about you. He did not even say a single word about you. Neither did I ask anything about your relationship," Piyali said.

"He did not even tell me that he called you," Sana said. "He always shares his all activities with me."

"Leave all this aside. Tell us about you. How many days in a month are you dating?" Kavita asked.

"Once in a month. My mom has strictly limited my date with him once in a month," Piyali said. "She thinks if I go for a date or spend a night with him, I will be pregnant."

"Tell aunty that it needs time and patience to be pregnant," Sana said. All of them could not stop laughing at this. And the conversation went on.

The next day Sana went to the office alone. Kavita informed her that she was not well. Sana did not know what was happening because she had seen Kavita too busy in the past few days on her mobile. She could not understand why Devraj was giving her so much time in these days. Though it made her happy to see her friend happy, but she was suspicious.

"Something is wrong," Sana said to herself, sitting in her allotted place.

She avoided making many friends in the work place. As Kavita was not there, she began to feel bored.

She pulled her mobile from her bag and thought to make a call to Kavita to ask if she was all right. She dialed her number. The mobile rang, but there was no answer from Kavita. The call went unanswered. She called twice and getting no response, she started working.

While coming back, Sana saw Kavita and Rudra walking towards a restaurant. She could not believe her eyes. She cross-checked again to confirm. She tried calling again, but Kavita did not respond.

"Don't do this Kavita," Sana said to herself.

Sana had seen Kavita too busy texting. She had thought it was Devraj, but now she could see what Kavita was cooking all these days. She did not like it. She had always believed in the divine relationship of love.

Sana went to her room, having many thoughts on what she will tell Kavita. She waited for Kavita to be back.

It was eight in the night when Kavita returned.

"Where were you?" Sana asked.

"Why are you so serious?" Kavita asked, smiling.

"Don't do it Kavita. You are doing something wrong," Sana said.

Kavita was shocked. She did not want Sana to know about her new relationship.

"We just went for a movie," she came directly to the point. She knew by Sana's voice that she was caught red-handed.

"You lied to me all these days. I thought you had been busy

with Devraj," Sana said. "I am ashamed of you."

"Don't be a typical girl," Kavita said. "What wrong did I do? I had gone for a movie with him."

"No one does anything wrong intentionally, but it happens," Sana said. "You are cheating on Devraj. I have seen how you remain stick to your phone these days and how you have started avoiding Devraj."

"What is your problem?" Kavita asked. "I just want to enjoy my life."

"Devraj loves you truly," Sana said.

"So, do I," Kavita replied.

"Yeah, I can see it," Sana replied.

"The problem is you do not know how things are going these days. Devraj does not have time for me. He is busy with his work. Have you seen since last few months him talking to me more than ten minutes?" Whenever I call him, he says he would call later, and I am tired of his avoidance."

"A relationship does not always remain the same. You cannot expect it to be as it was in the first few months of your relationship. You will have ups and downs and you know it."

"I am tired of his ignorance and his busy life," Kavita said.

"Kavita don't forget that your families had agreed on your relationship," Sana said and came close holding her hand. "This ring, do you remember?"

"I don't care about anything," she said and tried to remove it in anger, but she could not open it.

"You know what the actual problem is? It is because I am dating the guy who used to like you so much and you are jealous of it," Kavita said.

"Just shut up, Kavita. You are talking rubbish," Sana said. "A relationship of four years and you are paying it this way."

"Please stop," Kavita shouted. "Live your own life the way you like. Don't advise me. I know what I am doing. I like him, and I am dating him. Let Devraj be busy with his busy life."

Kavita had fallen for the guy. She could not even believe herself how it happened. Since the day she shared her number, they used to talk about Sana, but slowly they changed the topic. The late-night messages and avoidance od Devraj made Kavita fall for him and now she felt her love distributed in two parts.

Many a time when she heard about some girls dating two boys, she thought how enjoyable it was, and now when she was in the same position, she could see how difficult it was. She felt like neither she could leave Devraj nor Rudra, but life does not give you the chance of remaining in two boats at the same time.

CHAPTER EIGHT

Seven months passed, and Sana got a leave approval of fifteen days. She went home with a lot of plans. It was the second time she came home after getting the job, and now she was financially independent. She did not have to ask money from her parents to go out. She brought many gifts, and shopping for her parents.

"You have changed a lot," her mom said as she stepped into her house. Sana's parents were full of pride at this moment. They have successfully educated their daughter and made her independent. Finding an independent girl at that time was impossible, but Sana could make it to that point.

"Now don't say I have gained weight," Sana said as she hugged her mom.

"No mother ever has said this to their child even though if they gained," her mom said and smile.

"I missed you so much mom," Sana said. "Where is dad?"

"He went somewhere," her mom, said keeping her bag aside.

Sana sat on the bed, and her mom kept looking at her.

"What?" Sana said, raising her hand.

"It's been so long you were away," her mom said. "Our home remains empty without you."

"Mom now I have come home, so don't talk like this. I will always come every few months," Sana said. "I will fresh up now. Give me something to eat."

Sana went to the washroom, and her mother made ready the food she had cooked for her.

Her mom brought the dish which she had cooked early and placed on the table in her room. Her mother waited sitting on her bed.

"You always make this awesome meal," Sana said, lifting a spoon full of the stuff.

"Water is still dripping from your hair," her mom said. "Why don't you wrap your hair with the towel?"

Sana did not bother, she continued eating. It was her habit since her childhood. She never dried her hair after bathing and half of her clothes would wet with the dripping water.

"I think we got a guest," her dad said, smiling as he returned.

Sana looked back and smiled to see her dad. A glow on her face appeared. The glow of happiness and the seven months away from them could be read out from her face.

"Didn't your mom scold you for this," her dad said, pointing her wet untidy hair.

"Dad don't blame mom," she said, smiling.

"Oh, now that I was not at home during your arrival, mom and daughter have teamed up," her dad said in an artificial serious tone as if he was playing a role in b grade class Bollywood movie.

"It's not the right time to make a team or something. How is your work?" her mom asked.

"Before I say anything, let me open my bag," Sana said and lifted the bag on the table. She opened the bag and took out the stuff she had purchased for her parents.

"Here it is," she took out the mobile. It was her dream to get a mobile to her parents so that they could call her whenever they wanted.

"This is for you," she handed over a Panjabi to her dad.

"Why do you have to spend your money in all this?" her dad said.

Sana did not speak and kept searching in her bag and pulled out a saree for her mom. She handed over the saree. She had always seen how her mom used to compromise on her dress when they used to go for shopping. Many of the time, Sana's mom used to reject clothes, however, Sana discovered that it was because of color and cost preference. So, this time, she had purchased the most prefered color and designed saree for her mother.

"But we don't know how to use a mobile?" her dad said.

"Dad, I am home for fifteen days," she said.

***

"Oh my god, you have become so sexy," Piyali said. "Transformation, ha."

"Shhh… Sana said, putting her forefinger in her lips. "Dad is in the next room. Low down your voice."

"Transformation has occurred in you, not me. Look at you. You were different before the engagement and now look at you," Sana said, pointing her after a pause.

"You have grown too naughty," Piyali said.

"I think your hubby has worked much on you," Sana said, smiling.

"Whatever, your happiness can be read out from your face," Piyali said.

"So is your's," Sana replied.

"Let me know how it is going with Samar?" Piyali asked and sat on the bed with the pillow on her lap.

"Talk in a low voice. You know how my mom is sharp. I don't want anyone to know about it now," Sana said, hitting her back.

"I told you to come to my house. We could talk freely," Piyali said.

It was in the evening. Sana had called Piyali to her house. They sat in Sana's room. They knew they had to discuss many secrets, so they had closed the door. They always shared secrets in a closed room, and most of the time, it had been this room.

"I have many doubts, about Samar. Regardless of all the doubts I have badly fallen for him. He is such a great person," Sana said, closing her eyes and shaking her head sideways. It was as if she could feel him when she talked about him.

"So, you achieved your Arzu Siddiqui," Piyai said, smiling. "But what do you doubt about him? You are giving irony answers. You have doubts, and you have badly fallen for him. I am not getting you Sana," Piyali said. The relation between 'doubts' and 'badly fallen' made her to deep into the topic. She remained perplexed.

"I had asked him many a time if we could meet, but he had agreed now, after so many months. This Saturday we are going to meet, but I can't see any excitement in him. It seems due to my consistent force he is coming to meet me," Sana said, and her voice began to break. Sana wanted to see craziness in Samar to meet her just like many boys do before meeting their girls for the first time.

"Hey," Piyali said, giving a jerk holding her both hands. "You are overthinking. Why don't you take things positively? But finally, he is coming to meet you. Some boys are stubborn. You know that. You can change him after you meet him."

In every relationship, one person becomes dominant, but it varies. It is difficult for an observer to say who is dominant unless you are a close friend of one of them. Two persons cannot love each other with the same extent. The person who loves more gradually becomes the victim of dominancy.

"I have never felt the excitement in him compared to mine. I do not understand him. Sometimes I feel like he is the perfect person for me, the way he talks to me makes me feel great. His way of talking, his respect for me is huge," Sana said.

Piyali started smiling, and slowly, the intensity of her laughter was increasing.

Sana was confused by her reaction. "What makes you laugh?"

"The way you speak. You don't know what you are speaking," You have fallen for him badly, and there is no any doubt. It's all because you have started loving him so much that your expectations are beyond imagination. Your borderless love makes you think all this."

Sana could not understand what she was speaking. She was

blaming Samar for not showing his interest to meet her at the same time she was supporting him for his love. She was like saying he loves her, but he does not care for her and there is no such situation where a person can love, but not care for the person.

"Let me tell you the truth," Piyali said. "What I feel from your discussion is that he loves you so much. If a person can respect his girl enough then it would be wrong to say that he does not care for her. It's all about time."

Love is like a dormant seed. It needs time to germinate and then grow into a tree that bears the beautiful flowers.

"What are your discussions going about?' Sana's moms entered the room with two cups of coffee. "It's been so long you both were in the room."

Sana was afraid to see her mom suddenly. Her heartbeat rose.

"Nothing much, we were discussing about her marriage?" Sana said, pointing Piyali.

"Take coffee and continue your planning," her mom said, and she went out of the room.

"Ufff….," Sana took a deep breath and her heartbeat began to slow down.

"Don't be a kid Sana," Piyali said. "Why are you afraid so much?'

"I don't want mom to know anything at the moment. We know it is normal but for our parents, to fall in love is an offense," Sana said.

"But they will come to know someday," Piyali said.

"Everything has prescribed time, you know," Sana said.

"So day after tomorrow you are going to meet him," Piyali said. "What is the plan?"

"You and I will go to receive him," Sana said as she got more excited. "I don't know how I should dress?"

"Where should we go and where is he coming from?" Piyali asked.

"To the station, he will be coming by 6 in the evening," Sana said.

"No, I won't go with you," Piyali said and stood from the bed. "I have a plan for you. She began to discuss walking to and fro within the room. She wanted to make the first meeting the most memorable for Sana.

"We are not going to kidnap him," Sana said looking at Piyali. "Don't think too seriously."

Piyali laughed back at her.

"What type of dress does he want to see you in?"

"I do not know but I think jeans and Kurti," Sana said.

"All right! You should be at your best. I will be there waiting for you two in the nearby restaurant that falls just before the entry of the station. You will wait in the station with a bright smile on your face," Piyali said.

Sana began to imagine the scene. Her excitement increased further. She was smiling within. Imagination gives the best feeling. It brings the smile from your soul, and it is the best smile a person can enjoy ever.

CHAPTER NINE

"I will meet you on the way," Piyali said on the phone. "Drop me a text when you start."

Sana had planned that Piyali would come to her home, then move together at the station. She had thought to ask Piyali how she looked with the desired dress of Samar. But Piyali had decided to accompany her on the way.

Sana dressed at her best. She looked through the mirror, viewing herself at different angles. She tried all make-ups that would give her an attractive look. She had curled her hair from the beauty parlor the day before when she had gone shopping with Piyali. When the first crush becomes your first lover, you know the height of excitement, more so, when you are going to meet him for the first time.

"You should meet me in the way in ten minutes time," Sana said with her mobile in between her ear and shoulder as her hand was busy arranging back the stuff she used.

"All right," Piyali said and disconnected the call.

Sana stepped out of her room. "I may return late," she told her mom. She walked slowly step by step. Every step made her feel like bringing her closer to Samar though Samar had not arrived.

Samar had promised her in the night before that he would get the first train of the morning and most probably would reach the station by 6 pm. He had also shared his ticket and train details.

Sana checked the time on her watch again and again. She walked little further where she met Piyali.

"Awesome, you look awesome," Piyali said, looking at her. She pulled some of her hair from both sides to in front of her shoulder. "Now it's best."

"Thanks," Sana said.

They began walking together, talking about the plans they have made. When they reached the restaurant, Piyali said, "I will wait here. While you bring him from the station, I will join you here. And don't forget to call me when you get here with him," Piyali said and gave a wide smile. "Now go."

Sana strolled. The station was a walk of five minutes from the restaurant, Sana checked her watch, it was 5.50 pm. She walked to the station and stood, folding her hands. She wanted this to be the best day of her life. Every moment of waiting for Samar now seemed long. She looked around, and when the hour hand hit six, she heard the horn of a train. Her heart began to beat first. She could see the engine approaching from a distance. When it came closer, there was a rush. Some people were running towards the engine, and some were running towards the end of the train. No one bothered about anyone. They just wanted to get in or out of the train.

She looked at all the coaches where her sight could reach, but she could not see Samar. She walked from the engine to the last coach, but there was no sign of him. She searched in the crowd, but there was no face she could match with Samar of her imagination. She thought because it was Samar's first time at this station, he might not have known the exit. She walked again throughout the platform, but there were only crowds of unknown faces. She stepped back and thought to wait until the crowd becomes thin. Her eyes remained fixed to the people passing by her side as she sat near the exit. When the crowd had separated, she became hopeless and took out her mobile. She could see a message. She opened the message, and it was from Piyali. *Abdominal pain. Going back to my room. Call me when you return. Sorry.*

She looked at the message and ignored it. She dialed Samar's number, but his mobile was out of reach. She thought his battery might have dead as it was a long journey. She didn't know what to do.

"Where are you Samar?" she asked, looking at the empty station. "I am waiting for you. Meet me now or call me."

Depression hovered over her. Her eyes filled with tears. "No, he can't do this to me. He is not a person of breaking a promise."

Waiting for about twenty more minutes and seeing passed the other train; she stepped out of the station. She prayed to God that some miracle should happen. She remembered one episode of the series of Arzu siddiqui where he gave a surprise to his girl by coming to her at a sudden. He should come from back running calling out her name. She smiled with her full tear eyes still looking the crowds. No miracle happened. Neither Samar came running to her, nor did he come calling out her name. Sana knew life was not a story written by a person who loves only happy ending.

***

Twenty seven minutes ago

As Sana walked towards the station, Piyali entered the

restaurant. She did not come to the restaurant for food. She came to wait. She wanted Sana to meet Samar alone. In the absence of known people around, they can express their feeling in a better way that had since the last few months. She knew Samar would not express anything in the presence of her. So, she forbade Sana to accompany her till the station.

"One coffee please," Piyali said as she looked for a chair.

The excitement of Sana made her happy. She was curious now to see them together. She had seen the desire of Sana for Samar. She checked the time but it was just fifteen past six. She did not know how long they would take to come there.

Piyali took the first sip of the coffee when her mobile rang. She pulled out the mobile from her bag, and it was Samar calling.

"That's too early, you are in the right time," Piyali said and received the call.

She thought Sana had met Samar and they were coming. She began to take a quick sip to finish the coffee as she never wanted to make them wait for her on their special day.

"Hi," Samar said.

"Did you like her?" she asked. "She is just an angel."

"What are you talking about?" Samar asked in surprise.

"Now, don't act. I am talking about Sana," she said.

"What do you mean? I can't understand anything," he said, extending his confusion.

"Where are you?" she asked.

"I am at home," he said casually.

"You did not meet Sana?" she asked, keeping her cup of coffee aside.

"Why should I go? I have my own work," Samar said. "Why should she come to meet me at a sudden?"

"Wait, you mean you never talked to Sana. All these few months you did not talk to her?" Piyali said in surprise.

"No," Samar said casually. "Why, what's wrong?"

"What the hell are you talking," Piyali murmured. She could not understand what was happening. Many thoughts passed by her mind. Did Sana lie to me? Why would she lie? She had been discussing with me throughout these eight months, and every time she told me she was in love with Samar. No, she can't lie to me. I know her since childhood. But then why is it happening.

She was disappointed now. She thought and justified that Sana had lied to her. She thought whenever Samar had called her; he never said anything about Sana. She felt both of them were playing game with her.

She texted Sana and stepped towards her home.

\

CHAPTER TEN

Eight months ago

Samar, a charming young man from Shillong, was a simple, straightforward person. None could say where he was from. Since childhood to his higher secondary, he had to change school seven times not because he was someone who was thrown out of every school but due to his father's job. Till the time he had completed his standard five, he was in the fourth school from the list of the seven. The first three schools were within the seven sisters and the later in his class six his parents moved to Pune followed by Kolkata and finally to Guwahati.

The frequent shifting of schools did not affect much his education life, but it affected his personal life. He had made good friends, but when it had reached a time of making a big step in the friendship, time of shifting to another place arrived. Due to this reason, he had initiated many love stories which could not grow more than a year, hence leading to immature death of his love. Once he shifted, it was challenging to remain in contact because, the digital world had not developed too well in those days. The underdeveloped stage of the digital period, however, could not affect the true lovers because feelings were strong in those days. But memories many times sucked his tears.

"I cannot come to the party. I am swamped these days with

loads of work as examinations will begin soon," Samar said over the phone. He was busy typing the question paper.

Samar changed his job twice. He could not find job satisfaction, and finally, he decided to take up teaching.

As it is said if one of the parents is a carrier of a disease, then he or she may transmit it to their offspring. His father could not find job satisfaction even after changing jobs many times and so did happen with Samar.

Eventually, he joined as an assistant professor in the state university. It was just three months of his job when a new lady lecturer was appointed.

"We have gathered here to discuss marks allocation to the students while evaluating the papers," said the principal of the college.

It was a rule of the college that every year before the beginning of the examination, there was a meeting attended with all lecturers. The objective of the meeting was to ensure that the rules of the college are followed.

"I can't see our new lecturer, Jenny. Where is she?" the principal asked.

"I am going to call her," Samar said and walked out of the meeting hall.

Since the day Jenny had joined the college, Samar did not interact much. He was too busy with his routine work. As he walked to the teacher's common room, he could see Jenny, seated lost in her world of thoughts. She sat on the sofa with cross legs; her half hair was touching the hand of the couch. Her hand taking the support of the arm of the sofa was on her chick.

Jenny did not notice that Samar had come to call her for the meeting.

"Hey," Samar called.

She removed her hand from her chick. She pushed back her hair behind her ear.

"Yeah," she said.

"We got a meeting," Samar said. "Let's go."

"Sorry, I almost forgot," she said and stood to walk to the hall.

Samar could see teardrops in her eyes. He did not understand what she was going through. He stepped to the meeting hall along with Jenny.

"Please do not go for quantity of the answers," the principal began to discuss the rule. "Sometimes, two lines of an answer is equivalent to the answer of one page. I am not encouraging to give the same marks to the two-line answer and to a one-page answer, but I want you to assess the answer. In looking for a long answer, sometimes we leave behind the talent."

Whether it made sense or not all the faculty nodded their head.

The meeting ended in forty-five minutes and all dispatched. Samar was in thought about the tears in Jenny's eyes. So he walked to Jenny.

"Are you all right?" he asked.

Asking the question, he felt embarrassed because not knowing a person very well and asking directly about her condition.

No matter how well you know about a person, you can always approach to care for the person.

She turned and looked at him.

"I am fine," she said.

"I thought something is disturbing you," Samar said.

"My dad is in serious condition with his diabetic condition," she said. "He is diabetic since fifteen years."

"Oh. I am sorry," Samar said.

Samar stopped. He felt sorry for her. He turned back while she walked away.

***

"Do you want to take home your work?" Samar asked.

"I don't want but see these piles of papers are yet to be evaluated," Jenny said.

The examination had ended, and the works of students were now over. It was the time of hard work for the lecturer. No marking scheme was allowed to move out of the college campus, and marking was to be completed within college in a time frame which was strict.

Samar had just completed the evaluation. He was quick and did not think much to give marks. But it was not so with Jenny. She evaluated each with her full attention and sometime, taking help from the book to refer the answers because some answers confused her.

"Let me help you," he said and occupied the chair near Jenny.

Few of the lecturers looked at him as if he had committed a big mistake by asking her to help. He has worked the whole day to complete his task, and now he was ready to help Jenny.

Helping the person you like seems to be the most energetic activities you enjoy despite your tiredness. A normal human brain is always desperate for love.

"Thanks," Jenny said, keeping her focus on the paper and her pen.

Samar began the evaluation in, and no time he reduced the pile of half, and this surprised Jenny.

"Try to be fast," he said, looking at Jenny.

"Not everyone is gifted like you," she said.

"I wish I would be a gifted person," he said.

In another half an hour, both completed the evaluation and walked out of the college.

"I need a strong coffee," Samar said. "Let's go to that tea stall."

They walked, but the tea stall was closed. He was a caffeine and nicotine addict.

"Why don't we go to my room and make some strong coffee," Jenny said.

"A better option," he said with a smile. "But I do not want to spoil your room."

"What do you mean?" she asked.

"You know I need this too," he said, showing his cigarette packet.

"It's ok, you can light it in my room," she said.

They walked to her room. Everything in the room was so placed that it seemed no one lived there. Her sense of designing the room and arrangement was beautiful.

She entered and closed the door. Samar was uncomfortable to be in the room with her. He had never faced such situation and his face revealed his discomfort.

"You can sit on the bed," I will make coffee for you. "Make yourself comfortable."

"Yeah," he said and sat slowly on the bed. He did not know what to talk. His discomfort swallowed all his words, and indulged a fear in him of what people or other colleagues would think.

"Why are you so silent?" she asked, adding the coffee powder to the cups. She walked and sat beside him. "Here is your coffee."

"Thanks," he said and lifted the cup to take the first sip.

"You can light your cigarette," she said.

"Yeah," he said and pulled out the packet from his pocket. He lit the cigarette. "You are very organized."

He paused and thought if he said the right word. He thought she might now think that he was staring all round her room.

"Thank you," she said.

In a while the room became cloudy with the smoke and Jenny started coughing.

Samar stood and threw the cigarette away. "Sorry."

"It's not because of the smoke," she said, smiling.

"I think I should leave now," he said.

"All right," she said. "By the way thanks for the help."

"You make good coffee," he smiled at her and left.

Jenny closed the door and smiled. There was something she liked about him. She liked when he quickly threw away the cigarette for her discomfort.

Samar walked towards his house. He felt good having that strong coffee. He regretted lighting the cigarette in her room.

A few weeks passed. They became good friends. They had shared their past histories. They would always be together from going for work of off to home.

Being single, it is very difficult to not fall for the person you are always with.

"I think I have started liking you," Samar texted on the 20th day.

Samar had dined with her in her room. She had made some special dishes she was familiar with.

"Shut up," she replied back.

Samar could not understand what the meaning of the reply was. He was not afraid, but he could not think what next, he was going to text her.

It is very difficult to bring out the real meaning of the messages from the girl in your initial days with her.

"You didn't say anything about the food," she said.

"You are awesome," he said.

"What!!!" she said.

"I mean you are an awesome cook," he said.

"I think your mind is reflecting to you your crushes," she said. "Thinking about them you are typing."

"I never said I had crushes, I had said I HAD a crush in you," he replied.

"That girl, Piyali's friend," she replied.

"She was my crush three years ago. Crush does not mean love," he said.

Samar really did like Sana but he did not know her name. He always mentioned her as Piyali's friend. He had even approached, once but something stopped him. He felt keep it as secret.

Every person had some secrets that they never reveal.

"You still remember her," he said. "Your memories are too strong."

Something which you like and hate will always be in your mind.

As Sana was his crush, Jenny did not like it. The talking about her seemed to be Jenny the most ugly thing of the world.

"That's why I have taken up this profession," she replied.

"If I say I love you, would you mind?" he texted.

There was no reply for a while. She was dumb. Her hand trembled. She typed, but again deleted.

"I think you are drowsy. Sleep now."

"Then the answer is yes, I take it," he texted. "Good night."

She stood from her bed and began to walk in her room. She

looked at her mobile if the next text was coming. She knew she liked Samar and was in love.

"Are you asleep," she texted back in a while.

Samar did not reply. He read the text and smiled. He kept the mobile on his chest and remained silent smiling. He knew what was going through Jenny. He was assured that she would return with some answer.

"If I say, I would mind, what would you do?" she texted again.

She knew Samar was not asleep. She also knew that Samar was also in the same feeling that she was in.

"Then I will not say that I LOVE YOU," he texted.

His heartbeat increased. Though he was familiar with texting her but now it really excited his mind.

"Shut up," she texted.

Did she mean 'yes' by this reply? He questioned his inner thought.

"I never knew before that 'shut up' has the meaning of 'I love you too.'"

***

The following day Samar was not well, so he was on leave. He stayed back in his home resting. Every few minutes he was getting a message from Jenny. He was happy; he had someone who cares so much for him. While texting back Jenny, he got a call from an unknown number. He received the call and a beautiful voice from the other end spoke out, "Hi."

"Who is this?" Samar asked.

"We met in the party last week," unknown voice said. "Do you remember?"

Samar could not recall the voice. He did not even know if he had visited a party since six months. He was in confusion trying to guess some of his friends who might have called years later.

Asking further he came to know that she was the friend of Piyali. He could recall the face but he did not know the name though he had asked Piyali about her, but Piyali never revealed Sana's name to him.

No matter how little you know about your crush, no one can take up that place.

Suddenly he flashed back to the past when she used to be his crush. He liked her so much.

In a while he ended the conversation as he knew Jenny would be back to her room.

He could not believe what the consequences of the conversation with Sana would be. His heartbeat again began to beat with the same frequency as it used to beat when he first saw Sana. He knew he was taken but he wanted to make her friend as making friend is never harmful. However, he kept it away from Jenny as he knew Jenny would never accept it.

He had seen how Jenny gets jealous whenever he talked about Sana. He felt good to talk to Sana. He wanted to remain a friend.

Friendship before proposal and after break up will eventually lead you to fall for the person again.

Days passed and Samar made it a routine to talk to Sana. He started liking the way she talked. He could feel the desire in Sana's word to meet him, but he always had made some excuses not meet. As Sana did not reveal her name, he gave her the name Riya after actress Riya sen.

Finally, one day he could feel that he had already fallen for Riya (Sana). He did not want to cheat on Jenny. He loved her too and the days became very tough for him. Sometime he cried within himself. Neither did he inform Jenny about Sana, nor did he inform Sana about Jenny. He was depressed. He was left with no option.

"Punish me oh God," he said, being frustrated. "I don't want to live this life."

When a girl becomes suspicious, she will never stop her investigation till she finds the reality. And the final day when Samar had decided to go to meet Sana, Jenny became aware and she did not let Samar know about it. She was dying within her. It was unbelievable for her, but she was ready to let not Samar start this relationship.

"I have planned for a secret party tomorrow," Jenny said.

"I have some urgent work the next two days. So we will do it later," he said with a fake smile.

"Are you going somewhere?" she asked.

"Why do you think so?" he asked.

"Your tickets told me," she said.

Samar was shocked as he was unaware that he had the tickets in his bag, which he carried to college.

"I didn't want to make you feel bad," he said, trying to please her.

"Something is wrong," she said. "These days you always remain in your home. Your phone is busy most of the time."

"Do you doubt me?" he asked, trying to be serious.

"I do not doubt you, but I don't want you to go anywhere this month," she said.

"Don't be child Jenny," he said. "I have some work."

"Why can't you explain me your work?" she said loudly. Her face was red. She breathed heavily. Her eyes turned furious.

Samar sat on her bed, kept his hand on his head and remained silent.

"Fine, if you want this I won't go," he said. "I will leave now."

He went back to his home. He could not understand what he should do. He thought to call back to Sana and inform her. He searched for his mobile but it was missing. He searched his entire house but it was missing.

He came back to Jenny's room but Jenny informed him that she did not find his mobile.

Jenny was very angry. When she had seen the mobile, she checked the contact log and was surprised to see the call duration with the girl named 'Riya.' She had stepped on the mobile several times as if she was stepping on the face of Samar's Riya.

Eventually, Samar had to cancel his trip. He could not inform Sana that he was not coming.

Sana remained waiting in the station for him.

CHAPTER ELEVEN

The whole night passed, but Sana could not sleep. Her eyes were blood red with tears. Since the time she had come back from the station, she kept on trying to call Samar, but every time she tried to call, it did not go through.

"Why are you doing this to me Samar?" she said though there was no one in her room. It was 3 in the morning, and nothing could calm her.

Two thoughts hit her mind. She thought whether something had happened to Samar or he is trying to avoid her. She could not accept that Samar could avoid her, so she concluded that Samar might have been involved in some accident.

She continued walking in her room. She thought to call Piyali, but thinking about how she left her alone in the station made her feel egoistic. Gradually, morning arrived. Her pillow was half wet with tears. She washed her face to mask the depressing look and put on a fake smile, to hide the feeling from her mom.

It was just 7 am when she got a call from Piyali.

"What's up, buddy?" she said, jokingly.

"Why have you called?" Sana said.

Piyali could feel the pain in her voice. She wanted to tell her something important, but she hesitated.

"Can you come to my home?" Piyali asked.

"No, I am sorry," Sana said. "I will talk to you later."

"Wait ...wait don't disconnect the call," Piyali said. "Please come to my home by 10. I have something to inform you."

"What is so important?" Sana said in a suspiciously.

"Please do come," Piyali repeated. "We need to talk about Samar."

When Piyali pronounced the name Samar something suddenly hit Sana. She did not want to take it as her mind was thinking, but she had seen many cases of such types where friends become the main reason of the conflict between the two partners.

Sana did not want to go, but she couldn't avoid as it was related to Samar.

Sana reached Piyali's home at 9.55 am. She knocked the door and waited.

Piyali opened the door and she was shocked to see Sana's condition. She was so pathetic.

"Tell me what you wanted to say," Sana said as soon as Piyali opened the door.

"Come to my room," Piyali said, and started walking.

Sana walked to her room. On entering her room, Sana could not believe her eyes. She was confused whether she should scream with joy or fight with Piyali. Her eyes remained wide open. Her heart began to beat faster.

She saw Samar in Piyali's room. She did not know whether Samar had come to give her a surprise or is there something going between Samar and Piyali.

Sana stood in shock. She could not see any response from Samar.

Samar remained seated without talking a single word. He did not smile even when he looked at Sana.

Sana had come across Samar only in the engagement program of Piyali. Whatever the reason he was here for Sana remained nervous. She was filled with mixed feeling of surprise and happiness.

"Why did you lie to me?" Sana said, facing Samar. "I have been waiting to meet you for all these months. You made many unfulfilled promises. Is there someone else in your life? Why arent' you speaking now?"

"Sana," Piyali, called out.

Sana turned and looked at Piyali.

"Now don't say something is going in between you two," Sana said.

"Stop it yaar," Piyali said, raising her voice. "He is not Samar you had been taking to."

"Wha.. wha.. what did you say?" Sana said, laughing.

"He is not Samar you are in love with," Piylai said.

"Oh come on Piyali. I am not a child. Have you even forgotten Arzu siddiqui?" Sana said.

Sana was in love with Samar because he appeared to be the character of her favorite tv serial 'Ishq me tere'. Piyali had shared the number of Samar and all these she had discussed her relationship with Samar and now Piyali was saying he was not that Samar.

Now she was assured that Piyali was playing some game with her.

"I know everything and let me explain the matter," Piyali said.

"Enough, Piyali. I don't want to hear a single word from you anymore. Please leave me alone. Let me do what I want to," Sana said and was about to step out of the room when Samar called her name.

"Sana."

Sana stopped. She turned and looked at Samar. She could not match the voice with the voice she had been talking to. She could not understand what was going with her life.

"Please say it once again," Sana said.

"You are taking Piyali wrong," Samar said.

After returning from the station the last evening, Piyali had discussed about it with Samar and also had requested him to help her to make Sana understand. She wanted to bring Sana out of depression.

Now Sana could clearly make out that it was not the voice she was in love with. She could see that it was the face for which she had fallen but the voice was different. *No, no it is not possible. Perhaps the network made some changes and presented the voice to me.*

"Piyali, what's going on?" she asked, almost breaking into tears.

"Sana I know I am responsible for all these. The day I shared you the number of Samar, I mistakenly shared the number of another

Samar. I have got two friends with the same name, Samar roy and Samar kar. He is Samar Kar," Piyali said pointing Samar. "The person that you had been talking to is Samar Roy. It was just my fault that I overlooked and shared you another number," Piyali explained with guilt as she knew it was a very big mistake.

"What are you saying Piyali," Sana said in shock. "I can't believe my ears." Sana could not stand upright. Her legs began to tremble. She was so broken that her physics failed and she sat on the floor.

She was in love with Samar Kar. She had not seen Samar Roy ever. She had talked to him all these days with the face of Samar Kar in her mind. She was in a situation where she was in love with the voice of one person and the face of another person.

"You are not the one I was talking to all those days," Sana said like a child, looking at Samar with tears in her eyes.

"Sana, calm down. Sometimes mistakes happen in life. Whatever has happened it's all due to a mistake, and it is not possible to go back to your past and make things right," Samar said adding, "Now that you are in love with that Samar, it is fine. Love can happen with anyone, you know it."

"It is not about falling in love with someone it's about… No no, leave it, you will not understand the situation," Sana said with half-broken sentences.

How could Sana tell him that she loved him and not Samar Roy. Whenever she talked over the phone, his face had played in her mind. He had always imagined Arzu siddiqui in Samar. But now how could she say she loved Samar Kar, but talked to Samar Roy? How could she say she was in love with the voice of Samar Roy and face of Samar Kar.

"Piyali, I don't know what I should do," Sana said as she walked towards the door. "I should leave now."

She walked away while Piyali kept on calling her.

"She is depressed," Samar said. "Go and help her."

"I don't know how to handle it… Oh God… what have I done," piyali said in a tense mood.

"Give me her number. Don't worry. I will try to make her understand. Moreover, I am still single," Samar said to ensure Sana that hope was still there to make Sana happy as she back in her old days.

***

It was a tough time for Sana. She could not resist the pain. She could not digest the fact of falling in love with the voice of a person and the face of another person.

She stood in front of her window. Her eyes filled with tears.

"Sana," Piyali called, reaching to her room.

Sana did not respond to her call. She remained looking through her window.

"We need to think about it. Listen to me," Piyali said. "Samar wants …,"

Piyali was interrupted by Sana, "Enough Piyali. You have played your part. Please leave me alone now."

"I am sorry Sana," Piyali said, adding "I haven't made the mistake intentionally. You know I also wanted that you talk to

Samar as he resembled your hero."

"I am not asking for any explanation. So, please I request you not to talk about it anymore," Sana said, folding her hand in front of Piyali.

"Samar Kar is still interested in you. Just talk to him once," Piyali said, coming near her. Piyali wanted to give her some comfort. She felt her pain. She wanted to do something that would reduce her pain as it was her mistake.

"What do you think about me? Do I look like the type of girl who always needs a boy by her side? I have many more heroes whom I admire, should I accept all people who appear similar to them. There is something called love. Do you understand what it is? I don't need anyone in my life. Enough of my life," Sana said.

"Sana, I am responsible for all these. Look at me," Piyali said, holding her arms. "I know you are in love with Samar Roy now. You haven't seen him yet. He too is a good person. Should I try to connect a call to him?"

"I had tried Piyali last night. Once it rang but he disconnected the call. I do not know what is happening in my life."

No matter how angry you are, if you love someone you will end up burying the anger and ego. Sana had tried to call him many times but to no response. She just wanted to ask him a reason why he was doing so.

"How will he feel if he knows that all these days, I have loved him thinking he is someone else? Whenever I think about his voice the face of Samar Kar appears in my mind. I want to inform him all about this. I can't cheat on him," Sana continued. "He might have already come to know about it. Before he ends up this relationship I want to apologize."

Piyali looked at poor Sana. Her pathetic condition brought tears in her eyes. It was excruciating to see Sana in tears.

"Let me try to call him," Piyali said and called up Samar Roy.

Fortunately, the call was received. Piyali turned on her loudspeaker.

"Hi Samar," Piyali said.

"Which Piyali are you?" a girl's voice from the other end came.

"I need to talk to Samar. Please give him the phone," Piyali said.

"Please don't ever try to call again in this number. I am Samar's girlfriend. I know you are calling to talk about Riya," Jenny said.

Piyali could not understand who Riya was. Hearing this, Sana broke into tears. It was like the last day of her life. Pain after pain. It was as if she was sandwiched with pain. She felt the voice of how Samar gave her the name Riya. The memories flashed in her mind when she used to talk to Samar from the coin booth.

"How can he do this to me?" Sana shouted.

"Sana, shhh shhh," Piyali said to stop her.

"Samar never told you," Piyali said. "He is in relationship with Sana since few months."

There was no answer from the other end. The call was disconnected. Piyali tried to call again, but now the phone was switched off.

She did not know what suggestion to give to Sana. Whatever

she tried to calm Sana intensified her pain. She began to think what she could do. She was afraid that Sana could take any major step at this time, so she remained with her. A little later when she saw Sana lied on the bed, she left for her home.

As Piyali reached home, Kavita called up.

"Hi, Piyali," she said. Her voice was heavy. "Did Sana meet Samar?"

Since the time Kavita decided to move on with Rudra irrespective of Sana's warning, they hardly interacted. Sana began disliking Kavita. So she had called up Piyali to know about Sana.

"Why is your voice heavy?" Piyali asked. Piyali did not yet know that Kavita had cheated on Devraj and was dating Rudra.

"Something is wrong, Piyali. We are not together now," she said.

Kavita was now living with Rudra. It had taken a month when she decided that she could spend her life with him after breaking a relationship of four years with Devraj. The changes that she could see in Devraj after four years, she could observe it in a few months with Rudra.

Some changes take place naturally no matter how deeply you love a person, and you should be ready to accept. When Kavita was caught dating Rudra, Sana had warned her, fought with her to not cheat on Devraj because the reason Kavita gave for cheating him was an avoidable act of boys. Within some days boys do change and it is a fact.

In return she had answered that Devraj was too busy with his work. He was not ready to give his time for her. But the same incident was now happening with her again and this time it was from Rudra.

"What do you mean? Did Devraj do something wrong?" Piyali asked in surprise.

"No, Piyali," Kavita broke down. "His busy life forced me to leave him I moved on with Rudra."

"I can't believe what you are saying. Sana never told me about this neither did you," Piyali said.

"The reason for which I left Devraj, is the same reason I will leave Rudra too. Why, are they all the same?" Kavita said.

Now Kavita could realize that Sana was not wrong to warn her. When Rudra hurt her, she missed Devraj. She knew Devraj would never accept her again.

"What should I do now?" she said.

"Kavita give time. Everything will be fine. Your problem is nothing as compared to Sana. She is really going through hard time. You should talk to her," Piyali said. "The person she had fallen for is not the person she was in love with." Piyali explained all about the incidents.

Kavita really felt too sorry for Sana. She knew how emotional Sana was. She immediately called Sana.

"Sana," she said and broke down. She cried loudly. Sana did not understand what was going on with Kavita.

"What's wrong?" she said in a heavy voice.

"I am sorry Sana. I did mistreat you. Forgive me please."

"We will talk about it some other time. I will talk to you later."

"Don't disconnect. I know you are also going through hard time. I came to know all from Piyali. Don't feel bad. We three will be together again and we will sort out," Kavita said and explained all about her relationship and problem with Rudra.

CHAPTER TWELVE

A Few months later

Indeed, rough time snatches everything but above all 'time heals.'

The scar remains and it does bleed at times.

Everything has its own time- a time to hold on, and a time to let go. It's the feelings that don't want you to accept the change, thus you find lost in the world of thoughts.

Time was healing Sana's wound, but slowly. The pain that she was in a few months ago decreased and sometimes she could afford laughing. However, sometimes she could feel a sudden pain, but she was optimistic that everything will be normal as she had already seen people who had bad break up living a happy life.

"Welcome," Piyali said to Samar Kar as he congratulated her. Samar has come to attend her marriage party.

Piyali and Kavita had planned a meeting to call the people around Sana and Kavita a day earlier to have extensive discussion as Sana always kept on saying, 'I wish one day Samar Roy explains to me the reason why he did this.'

Samar walked with her to the room where Sana and Kavita were busy in their discussion.

Samar Kar on the request of Piyali had called Sana many times in the last few months. Deep down, his desire for Sana was still alive. There was something which did not let Sana's soul to have Samar's feelings. She had developed love phobia.

Gradually, everyone gathered, and it was a huge surprise for everyone. No one wants to come face to face after a break up, but Piyali had brought all of them in one room.

Kavita and Rudra shared the sofa. Samar Kar, Devraj, Piyali, and Sana sat on the other side. Samar Roy occupied the other chair.

The room was fully packed. It was as if a secret meeting of the RAW agents was going on. There was a face of seriousness and fear that could be seen on Samar Roy, Rudra and a mask of depression on Sana and Devraj.

"Please, do not take anything that we discuss here personally," Piyali said. "I know it is astonishing for you to see these faces together. I had to keep this meeting a secret from all of you. I know you are all my guests today, but looking into the condition of my friends I will have to speak up."

Everyone was silent. Majority of them were guilty for something or the other.

Samar Roy looked into Piyali. He did not know everyone would be here and answer he has to answer for the betrayal. In fact, none of them knew that they were going to have something like this.

"I think we should start with Kavita," Piyali said, looking at her.

"Me??? Kavita was shocked. She never knew that she had committed a big mistake. She had given her the reason for retreating

Devraj.

"What should I say? We are good now," she said, looking at Rudra.

"Then what did Devraj do?" Piyali asked. "He should know the reason of you retreating?"

"Look Piyali, you have no right to talk about personal matter," Kavita said. "Now Devraj is happy with his life and I am happy with mine."

Everyone looked at Devraj who was listening keenly.

"Devraj, do you have something to ask?" Sana asked.

The ultimate aim of Piyali was to come to the topic of Sana because no one was in distress like Sana.

"I am happy that you are happy now," Devraj said, pointing Kavita. "I just want to know that how long had you been cheating on me?"

It was embracing for Kavita. Cheat is a word, but it definitely brought out the negativity of Kavita, she became uncomfortable.

It is not an easy task to speak the truth in front of your ex and current partner.

"What the hell is this?" Rudra said and stood in anger.

Everyone looked at him.

"Hey man, don't take it another way. You know how these things are disturbing these days. Nothing wrong to know the real truth," Samar Kar said, trying to calm him.

"Why don't you say everything?" Rudra said in a loud voice to Kavita.

Kavita remained silent.

"Ok, let me tell you," Rudra said. "I have been dating her since the time she joined her job. Initially, I did like Sana, but she did not talk to me. So I thought to take help from Kavita, but unfortunately, I fall for Kavita.

She had told me that she did not have anyone in her life, and we started dating regularly."

Tears filled Devraj eyes. He didn't want to show. So, he moved to the washroom and came a few minutes later. Devraj had many questions to ask. He knew nothing was going to change even after knowing why she did cheat, and instead, it might hurt her current relationship. So he remained quiet.

Piyali went out and brought tea.

"Samar Roy, you have to explain to Sana everything," Kavita said. "Why you did all this to such a nice person. I may not be good but Sana is always a pure hearted girl.

"I don't know how to apologize. I know it was a huge mistake," Samar Roy continued. "The day when Sana called me, she told me that we had met in the party but I know I did not attend Piyali's engagement party. I told her that I did not meet her, but her persistence led me to not give much importance on it and I continued talking to her. As you know Piyali, I did like her once, so I thought we would be friends. So, I had always made excuses not to meet her."

"But you never told me that you had a girlfriend, Jenny," Sana said.

Samar remained silent.

"So I can assume you never loved me," Sana said.

"Partially," Samar replied.

Sana laughed with a fake smile. But she felt happy as she had kept on blaming herself for loving Samar Roy with the face of Samar Kar. It was as if a huge burden of mountain came down from her shoulder and she was free now.

"Let me now explain to you why I did talk to you over the phone," Sana began explaining. "The day I had called you, I did call for Samar Kar. I thought you were Samar Kar. I did fall for you, but truly not for you, but for Samar Kar. I had a crush on him because he resembled my hero Arzu. Why didn't you come to meet? It really hurt me but when I came to know from Piyali that you were not the one, I laughed within me. I thanked God it happened like that."

Deep down, Sana knew she had fallen for him. If Samar would not cheat her, she would happily be living with Samar Roy forever.

Samar Kar felt happy hearing this. He had also started liking her.

"Please, drink your tea," Samar Kar said. "It's getting cold."

"I would like to apologize to you Sana," Samar Roy said. "I am getting married to Jenny in the next month and I wish all of you come to my marriage event."

"We do not want to have this RAW meeting again," Rudra said, laughing. "So, it is no from us."

"Piyali, are we done?" Samar Kar asked.

"Yeah, let's have launch. I am sorry if you felt something bad about this meeting," Piyali said and the meeting ended. Piyali helped them to shift to their allotted room for the night.

When everyone left the room, Samar Kar called Sana.

"Hi," he said.

"Are you going to start some fresh conversation?" Sana asked.

"Maybe it is about 'Ishq me tere," Samar said.

"I haven't watched the last few episodes. I miss it so much," Sana said.

"I have completed the last few episodes," Samar said. "If you are interested I can tell you the story," Samar persisted.

"Please go ahead," Sana said and changed her pose to comfort.

"Arzu is now alone," he said.

"Why? What happened to Sara?" she asked.

"After her leg was cut off to save her life, she was free from cancer, but she could not bear the pain of the guilt she had," he continued. "You remember when Arzu was abroad, she dated another boy."

"Yeah, I can never forget that story," she said.

"The guilt did not let her live. After few months of her surgery, she committed suicide," Samar said.

Samar felt good to see Sana listening attentively to his words. He wanted to talk to her. He was not a fan of the episode, but he knew Sana did like it, so he had collected information about the story till then.

"I did not like much that girl. She cheated on him," she said.

"Now Arzu is single," he said. "And so am I."

Sana smiled. She made real eye contact with him and she was smiling from her inner person.

"It's late, we should sleep now," Sana said. "We will talk later. A lot of work for tomorrow."

"Goodnight," she said with a bright smile. She began walking towards the door with a real smile, and full thoughts when Samar called back.

"Sana."

THE END